TIL DEATH DO US PART

Marriage Survives
The Stress of Military Life

VIRANDA I. SLAPPY

Printed in the United States of America

Library of Congress Control Number: 2017958483
eBook: 978-1-948172-00-4
Softcover: 978-1-948172-01-1
Hardcover: 978-1-948172-15-8

STONEWALL PRESS
PAVING YOUR WAY TO SUCCESS

Stonewall Press
363 Paladium Court
Owings Mills, MD 21117
www.stonewallpress.com
1-888-334-0980

SUMMER OF 1974

In the summer of 1974, in Bibb, Georgia, a pretty, brown-skinned African-American girl named Virginia Cottingham and her mother lived with her grandparents. Mrs. Cottingham had legally separated from her husband. That summer at the town's bowling alley, Virginia met a young black guy named Carlos Slaughter. Rose, Virginia's, pretty, long-haired friend was also at the bowling alley with other friends. Rose stayed close to her boyfriend Curtis while the rest of the girls talked among themselves.

Slaughter approached Virginia and laid one of his strongest raps on the 5-foot-4-inch seventeen year old. Virginia, however, was reluctant to talk or give any information to him. So Slaughter temporarily gave up the hunt. That is until he overheard Virginia and her friends moaned about being short seventy-five cents for a bucket of chicken that they wanted to take with them to Tobesofkee Lake. Slaughter quickly offered to give them the seventy-five cents in exchange for Virginia's telephone number. Virginia still refused to give out her telephone number to Slaughter, who at 5 feet 6 inches was only two inches taller than Virginia. Despite his height, Slaughter had a way with women. He had bow-legs, a gap in his upper front tooth, sported a small afro, and had a charming personality. Slaughter insisted, saying, "No number, no money."

Rose pulled Virginia aside and pleaded with her to give the guy her number. Saying, "We need the seventy five cents for the chicken. So what if you don't like him? You can feed him a line of lies when he calls you." Giving up, Virginia walked over to Slaughter and gave him her phone number in exchange for the seventy-five cents. The girls then brought the chicken and headed out to the lake.

Two days later, Virginia received a phone call from Slaughter who has had eyes for Virginia for a long time. He knew that she wasn't dating anyone because he was dating the cousin of the last guy that she dated. Slaughter had the inside story on Virginia's relationship with Teddy. A guy she had dated for three years before breaking off the relationship.

"What's up with you, Virginia?"

"Nothing. I was just sitting here looking at television."

Mrs. Cottingham yelled from the bedroom, "Who's on the phone?"

"It's for me, Mom,"

"So tell me, Virginia," said Slaughter. "How did it go at the lake?"

"Oh, we had a wonderful time."

"I started to come, but I didn't want to crash the party since I didn't have a personal invitation."

"You were welcome to come if you wanted to."

"Yeah, well that wasn't the impression that I got from you at the bowling alley,"

"Well, I'm sorry if I gave you that impression, but I usually don't give out my phone number to strangers."

"Well, I guess I'm just going to have to change that," Slaughter said in his most charming voice.

"Well, I guess you would if you can."

"Oh, I can and I will. Especially when there is something I like."

"Tell me, has anyone ever told you that you have some big, pretty eyes?"

"Yeah, guys always tell me that."

A week later, Rose called Virginia to tell her the stationery that the cheerleaders were going to sell to help raise money for new uniforms had arrived, and she was going to bring her share by the house.

The following Saturday, Rose brought over the stationery. She said that she just left Carrie's (also a cheerleader) house to drop off her share. And guess who's with Rose? Slaughter. He's taking her around to deliver the stationery. "Virginia, aren't you going to invite Slaughter in? I hate for him to wait in his car," said Rose.

"Sure, Slaughter can come in."

"You all have a fine place."

"Well think you Slaughter," said Virginia.

"Hi, Mrs. Cottingham, how are you doing?" asked Rose.

"I'm doing fine, Rose. I see you are bringing work for Virginia and me to do, huh!"

"Yep. We have to sell this stationery so we can buy some new uniforms," said Rose.

"Who is that with you Rose?" asked Mrs. Cottingham. "Is that your brother?"

"Oh, no, he's a friend, Mrs. Cottingham."

"Alright. I guess I'll leave you all alone so you can continue whatever it was you were doing," said Mrs. Cottingham.

"I will buy a box of stationery from you," Slaughter told Virginia. "Oh, good. Here's yours right now."

"I don't have the money on me now. Why don't I stop by at another time? That way I can offer to take you around the neighborhood to sell your stationery. I know you probably would get plenty of sales in my neighborhood."

"Okay, let's do that then."

Virginia and Slaughter started seeing one another but hadn't made a commitment. Virginia's mother was unsure of Slaughter's motives concerning her daughter, partially because he appeared much older than he claimed to be, though he had shown Mrs. Cottingham his driver's license. One day, Mrs. Cottingham received a call from Mr. Cottingham. He told her that Virginia's child support check was at his mother house. Mrs. Cottingham asked Slaughter who had stopped by if he would drive Virginia to her grandmother's house to get the check since she had no transportation to go herself. Slaughter was glad to do Mrs. Cottingham a favor. Plus, this would give him the chance to meet Virginia's grandmother and spend some time alone with Virginia. Slaughter offered to take Virginia to a movie after they had picked up the check. She accepted his invitation. Virginia forgot to lock the car door when she got out and walked with Slaughter into the

Bibb theater. Slaughter further forget to check the door, knowing that he had his clothes on the back seat.

Slaughter and Virginia were walking arm in arm to the car after the movie when he suddenly asked her, "Did you lock the door?"

"I can't remember locking your door," she replied.

At once, he released his arm from hers and ran to the car, hoping that his clothes were still there. Virginia noticed the change in Slaughter and wondered to herself why he was so concerned about his car doors. After all, he had just impressed her by appearing to have money to burn. Finding his clothes missing, Slaughter embraced Virginia and assured her that the loss was no big deal.

Slaughter had been calling on Virginia for sometime, and he felt it was time to make his move. He arranged a meeting place at his Aunt Lacey's, who had separated from her husband and lived by herself. Aunt Lacey had a date the day of Slaughter and Virginia's meeting and needed to borrow Slaughter's Pinto. He had everything in motion. The last missing link was getting Virginia to go out with him on that day. Slaughter called Virginia and she accepted his invitation to go with him to a party. Right after the phone call, Virginia went shopping for something special to wear. When she returned, Debra, her cousin, called to say that she was coming over to spend the night. Virginia okayed it, but told her that she wouldn't be there because of her date with Slaughter. She was unhappy to hear this, but decided to come anyway.

When Debra arrived, Virginia invited her to come along. Debra declined because she didn't have a date. So Virginia asked her to call her boyfriend and see if he would go with her. Debra called Walter, but he had to work. Virginia then insisted that she go with them anyway, saying, "Besides you may meet someone else."

"No, I don't want to go." Besides, Slaughter is not like Teddy or Michael for that matter. He's doesn't like to ride your friends around. Virginia, he's different from the others."

"Oh, Debra, stop being silly. Of course, he's not like the rest. He's different and there's something about him I like. And, although I don't know what it is yet, I'm going to hang in there until I find out."

"Well, go ahead and have fun," Debra insists. "I'll be waiting to see how your night went."

Slaughter arrived at seven o'clock on the nose. His eyes lusted for love, beaming and shining as he took in Virginia's radiance. Naive Virginia doesn't pay any attention to Slaughter's lustful eyes. She was too excited about going to this party and too concerned about her appearance.

At the party, Slaughter and Virginia mingled with people who was much older than they are. This surprised Virginia and she had mixed feelings at first. But later on, she began to relax and be sociable. Around eight o'clock, Slaughter asked Virginia if she was ready to leave. Virginia said that she was. The crowd was older than she had expected.

While driving, Slaughter ask Virginia, "Since the night still young, how about going with me to see my Aunt Lacey?"

"Sure. Why not? I'm not ready to go home yet."

After arriving, Slaughter introduced Virginia to Aunt Lacey. She was about thirty-one years old; plump, short, and had a high yellow complexion. As the two women sat in the kitchen talking about Slaughter and how they met. Aunt Lacey got a phone call and asked Slaughter if she could use his car. Slaughter, gladly gave his permission.

"You kids don't mind being here for a while, do you? I shouldn't be that long. You can go upstairs to the den and watch some television until I get back. There's some food in the kitchen; help yourself."

Slaughter asked Virginia if she wanted anything to eat.

"No, thank you. I'm still full from eating that food at the party," Virginia said.

Instead they went upstairs to the den and relaxed while looking at television. Slaughter slowly embraced Virginia and they kissed. As they kissed, Slaughter started to feel her petite, shapely, brown body. He said that he desired her and began slowly undressing her. Virginia responded but had mixed feelings. She wasn't ready for this---she was still a virgin. Slaughter continued to touch her passionately; rubbing and caressing her in all the right places. His goal was to make her feel relaxed so he could fulfill the burning desire he had to love her body.

Virginia's desires had overcome her. Slaughter had become irresistible to her. They undressed each other slowly. Slaughter rolled a rubber onto to his erect penis while Virginia watched; obviously fascinated by the sight of seeing her first erect penis. As Slaughter attempted to penetrate Virginia's vagina, she froze. She didn't want him to know she was a virgin. She held her legs slightly close together, praying he wouldn't realize that he hadn't entered her secret garden after all. Slaughter was so into getting some of that sweet thang that he didn't realize he hadn't penetrated her. Afterward, Slaughter admitted his feelings for her. Virginia, still having mixed feelings about what happened, admitted softly to him how she felt also. Moments later, they dressed, and Aunt Lacey returned and pulled Slaughter aside to question him about what had happened.

"We enjoyed a movie on TV. Thanks, Aunt," he said.

He returned upstairs to get Virginia, who was waiting in the den. When they got downstairs, he thanked his aunt again and drove Virginia home. Later, Virginia received a call from Slaughter. He told her how special this night was for him, hoping she felt the same. Virginia told him that she didn't have a good time and they didn't really make love because he didn't have his penis inside of her and hung up the phone. Debra overheard their conversation and asked Virginia if she was alright.

"Yes, I'm alright! No, I'm not alright," said Virginia in a rude tone. "Debra, Slaughter set me up. He had tonight planned from the beginning. He intentionally set out to screw me tonight. But I chickened out. I'm a virgin. I don't know how to fuck." She cried. "I had these sensuous feelings and desires one moment then when we were getting ready to do it, something came over me and I froze. I just couldn't go through with it. And the sad part is, he didn't realize his damn dick wasn't in me."

Debra grabbed Virginia and embraced her saying that everything is going to be alright. Virginia then calmed down. Debra said, "I need to ask you something. Did he use a rubber?"

"Yeah, he used one. That's why I believe he planned this night. However, this incident doesn't change how I feel about him, and I'm afraid that tonight, I've failed again as I failed in my relationship with Teddy. Debra, what's wrong with me? Why can't I be like the other girls? That's why Teddy went with someone else to fulfill his needs."

"Quit selling yourself short!" Debra exhorted. "I wish I were like you. Do you realize how many girls maintain their virginity? It is the hardest thing that a girl has to do. Besides, giving yourself to Teddy wouldn't have made any difference in your relationship. If he loved you, as he claimed he did, he would have waited until you was ready. You are confusing your relationship with Teddy with the one you're in now. Slaughter may have planned this night, but in your heart, you wanted to have sex as much as he did.

"Keeping your virginity is one thing; sharing it with someone special is another. You must decide what it is that you want in this relationship before you continue. I wished I had someone to share my feelings about sex with. I'm no expert, but my ears and my heart are here for you when you need me."

The ringing telephone interrupted Debra. It was Slaughter. He wanted to talk with Virginia. Debra placed her hands over the receiver and tried to persuade Virginia to talk with him. She reluctantly took the phone from her. Slaughter tried to convince Virginia that he still cared for her though nothing happened.

"It doesn't matter to me that you couldn't have sex or that we didn't actually make love. What matters is that I still love you and want to continue seeing you. When can I see you again?" he pleaded.

"That's just it. You can't. We haven't made a commitment to each other to continue this relationship."

"Okay, Virginia, you're right. I have not asked you to date me. So, will you start going out with me?"

"You mean you actually want to start going out with me after what happen tonight?"

"Yes, didn't I just ask you? Like I told you before, I've had my eyes on you long before you knew I existed. Now, that I've had the pleasure of getting to know you, I want to love you even more!"

Virginia cried tears of joy. She hung up the phone and cried out to Debra, "We, are officially dating one another!" Debra, although happy for Virginia, wondered if this guy right for her friend.

Virginia and Slaughter had been dating for about two months, when she ran into Norris Towers after school.

"Hey, Virginia what's up with you and Slang?" he asked.

"What do you mean what's up with me and this Slang? I don't know what you are talking about. I don't know anybody by that name," she said.

"Oh, so you don't know Slaughters' nickname?"

"What? You've got to be kidding me, Norris. I didn't know that Slaughter was called that." Slaughter called Virginia that same night after she ran into Norris. During their conversation she called him Slang. He became silent for a moment, then he said, "Who told you my nickname?" She then told him about my conversation with Norris. "He wanted to know whether or not we were dating, and he told me your nickname."

Slaughter and her had been dating for five months when he got the courage to plan another night to remember. This time, it was perfect. She had gotten the courage to tell Slaughter she was a virgin at his brother's house. This time, we made passionate love and it was good.

It was November of 1974, and each November, the military recruiting officers representatives visited the high school to recruit students for the military. The very day the recruiters came to the school to give their orientation on the different branches of service and what they had to offer, Slaughter decided that he wanted to join the Army. He arranged to have himself tested.

Christmas time was near and bells were ringing in the students' ears at Northeast High. All the lovers wondered what their loved ones were getting them for Christmas. Slaughter ran into Rose at school one day and quizzed her about what to get Virginia for Christmas.

"I have no idea. But I could find out for you if you would do the same with my boyfriend Curtis," said Rose.

Slaughter already knew what Rose was getting. However, he pretended not to know. Saying that's no big deal and he can easily find that out.

The next day, Rose saw Virginia at school and steered the conversation into a topic about Christmas gifts. Virginia said she would love to have an eight-track cassette player.

"Honey child, what do you mean you would love an eight-track cassette player? Do you know how much that would cost?" said Rose.

"Yes, I do." said Virginia. "Besides, Slaughter always flattered me with the impression that he has money, and that my desires have no limit. So that's what I want."

"So, tell me, Virginia. What are you getting him for Christmas?"

"I'm getting him a watch."

"A watch!" yelled Rose. "Where are you going to get that kind of money?"

"Since you really want to know, I told my mother that Slaughter was getting me an eight-track, and that I had to get him something nice in return."

"You mean your mother agreed to buy him a watch?"

"Yes, because if he gets me the eight-track, my mother won't have to buy one."

"Now, suppose Slaughter doesn't buy you a tape player? I would hate to be in your shoes when your mother finds out what you have done. Girl, you better pray he does have that type of money and love you enough to get it."

"I'm praying, too."

One week before Christmas, Virginia asked Slaughter what he wanted for Christmas. Slaughter kissed her on the lips and held her so close that she could feel his hard penis.

"You, baby," he said.

Virginia responded, saying, "It's me you shall have." And they had sex for the first time in Virginia's living room. After they finished their energetic romp, Virginia said, "I didn't mean for this to get out of hand." The door was closed and everyone was asleep, so their lovemaking went unnoticed.

"You know, Virginia, I think Mrs. Cottingham has finally accepted me and has gotten over Teddy," said Slaughter.

"I think so, too," said Virginia as she kissed his juicy lips.

"Well, it's getting late and I better be going before my mother starts wondering where I'm at. She doesn't know that I'm here. I came by here right after work."

Slaughter went to his room when he got home. He opened his dresser drawer, and picked up a small jewelry box. He opened it up and looked at the ring inside. He drifted off into deep thought and imagined the expression that he's going to see on Virginia's face when she sees it.

INTRUDER

Virginia was thinking about how much she loved Slaughter when the phone rang. She answered the phone, and, Teddy, her ex-boyfriend spoke.

"Well, hello, Virginia."

"Who's this?"

"How soon we forget someone who we promised to love forever."

"Teddy, it's you."

"Hey, baby it's me. The one and only. Obviously, you were expecting Slaughter. Yup, I heard you were dating him. I also heard that y'all were serious. Baby, you know that no one could ever take your place in my heart."

"Why did you call, Teddy? You have no business calling me anymore. We're finished."

"Baby, you and I will never be finished. I told you once and I'll tell you again: If I can't have you, no one else will. I still love you, Virginia. I always will. We're meant to be together. So what if you are seeing someone else? Baby, you will never say that you can forget what we had and how much we meant to one another. I passed by your house and had planned to stop by, but I saw Slaughter's car and changed my plans."

"So you decided to call me, huh? Suppose he was still here?"

"Baby, it hadn't been that long since we have seen one another. Besides,

I know Mrs. Cottingham's rules about you having company over. So tell me. Baby, when can I see you again? I need to hold you in my arms and whisper in your ears how much I miss you. I especially need to look into your big beautiful eyes. I want a chance to patch it up between us."

"Well, you can't. It's over."

"Baby, listen. That is what you want to believe. But, baby, you can't just throw away what we had. I told you that Wanda didn't mean anything and Betty Ann was a mistake. Baby, I know I hurt you, but my feelings for you never changed. I just had needs that you weren't ready to fulfill at the time. I respected you too much to impose my selfish needs upon you. Besides, I wanted you to be able to make love to me without any doubt. Maybe I respected you too much. I don't know how else to explain how I felt and the decision I made when it came to the sexual commitment for us."

"Well, I'm not going to fulfill your needs now either. Like I said, I have found someone else."

"Okay. You want to play hard to get. You believe this, Virginia, I'm back in town for Christmas break, and I will see you. So don't get too wrapped up with Slaughter because it's not over until I s ay it's over. Good night and sweet dreams 'cause Teddy is back. I still love you," he said before sending a kiss through the telephone. Virginia hung up the phone and looked so distraught that her mother asked her what was wrong.

"Mom, that was Teddy! He's home for Christmas."

"Baby, you have fear in your eyes. Do you still have feelings for Teddy?" Virginia glanced at her mother and said nothing while slowly walking away. Later that night, Virginia got a call from Slaughter.

"Virginia, I've been trying to call you for at least an hour. Who were you talking too?"

"Feeling depressed, she told him that it was Teddy. After taking a deep breath, she told him that he call to say hello, and that he was home for Christmas break."

"What did y'all talk about?"

"I told him that it's over, and that I love you, and that I didn't want him calling me again."

The next day, Slaughter went to the bowling alley hoping to run into Teddy. Meanwhile, Teddy has a temporary job working at Eddie's Men Shop. Teddy is working so he can get enough money to take Virginia out. Slaughter saw some of Teddy's hanging partners. They tell him that Teddy is back.

"Man, you know Teddy and Virginia had something strong going on for a while," Larry said.

"Hey, man I'm not worried about Teddy or anyone else for that matter. Virginia is my girl now," Slaughter said before leaving the bowling alley angry.

Teddy continued to call Virginia to tell her how much he cared. Virginia politely listens but continued to tell him that she's seeing someone else. Christmas day came and Virginia was nervous because she still doesn't know what Slaughter has brought her. She's hoping that it's an eight-track tape player. At Slaughter's family's house, everyone watched him wrap Virginia's gift. His mother can see in her son's eyes that he really loves Virginia and hope to marry her one day. His sister, Sheila, asked if he was giving her the gift here or at her grandmother's house.

"I'm going to pick her up and bring her over here," said Slaughter. "Boy, I can't wait until I see the look in her eyes when you give her

this," said Sheila.

"I can't either."

Slaughter finishes wrapping Virginia's gift and went to pick up his soon-to-be fiancée. Meanwhile, Virginia called his house, and Sheila said he had left to pick her up. Virginia nervously hangs up the phone. Her mother said, "Virginia, you should be excited, not nervous, child. Your hands are shaking. You already know what you are getting."

Ding-dong!

"Virginia, it's Slaughter." said Cousin Junior. "Hey, man, come in, merry Christmas."

"Man, merry Christmas to you too," said Slaughter. "Man, I was just about to ask Virginia about you."

"Hey, what are you all going to be doing later?"

"Man, I'm going to take Virginia over to my house to eat dinner."

"Well, man, if you all get a chance stop by my house. Maybe we all can get together later."

"Alright, man, I'll see about getting up with you later. Merry Christmas, Mrs. Cottingham."

"Merry Christmas to you to, Slaughter," said Mrs. Cottingham. "Virginia are you ready to go?" said Slaughter.

"Yes, but first, I want you to open your gift."

"Okay, I'll open it." Slaughter open his gift. "Baby, I really do like this. Thank you. Baby let's go, my family's waiting," Slaughter said as he hurried her out of the door.

"Mom, I'm gone!" yelled Virginia to her mother as she left with Slaughter.

At Slaughter's house, he and Virginia sat quietly in the living room. Virginia glanced at their Christmas tree and noticed there was no big box under it. Some gifts were open and but others were still wrapped. She waited patiently and wondered, where's my gift? I told my mother that Slaughter had gotten me the tape player.

"What are you thinking about?" said Slaughter.

"Oh, it's nothing! I was just admiring your mother's Christmas tree"

"I'm going to go to my room for a moment. Wait here until I come back," said Slaughter. "Okay."

Sheila, petite with a high-yellow complexion, came into the room and socialized with Virginia until Slaughter returned.

"So, have you had a good Christmas?" asked Sheila. "So far, I've had a wonderful Christmas."

"Tell me, girl, what did you get?"

"I mostly got clothes."

"Tell me, what did my brother get you?"

"He hasn't given me my gift yet, but I gave him a watch."

"A watch! Slaughter, let me see your Christmas present!"

Slaughter returned to the living room with a large box. Virginia's eyes gleamed with joy when she sees Slaughter bringing her present. Mrs. Slaughter, and his brothers and sisters gathered around Virginia, yelling, "Hurry up and open your present!"

"Okay, I'm going to open it right now," said Virginia. She unwrapped the first box only to find another one to be opened. Still excited, Virginia unwraps the second box, finding still another one. A little less excited, Virginia unwrapped the third box and still found a smaller one. Not feeling excitement—only disappointment—Sheila yelled to her to open the little box. Tears formed in Virginia eyes as she opened it. Inside was a jewelry box. Virginia, glowing with anticipation, opened it. "Oh, my God! It's an engagement ring!" she screamed. Virginia placed her hands over her mouth and stared at the ring in shock. Slaughter immediately grabbed the box and removed the ring. Then he placed the ring on her finger and said, "Virginia, will you marry me?"

"Yes, I will be glad to marry you," she said as they kissed passionately.

The two lovebirds left the house right after dinner. The meal Slaughter's mother prepared, as always, was delicious. When they arrived at Virginia house, Mrs. Cottingham noticed they didn't enter with a boxed gift. Mrs. Cottingham anxiously asked her daughter, "What did Slaughter get you?" Virginia was very excited but calmly showed her mother the engagement ring.

"Virginia, this is a beautiful ring. I never thought Slaughter was that serious about you." Virginia's brothers and sisters ran up to her and asked to see the ring.

"You mean you guys are getting married? Virginia, come with me for a moment. Excuse us, Slaughter, for one moment," said Junior as he took Virginia to their mother's bedroom. "I want to see if that's a real diamond ring."

"Oh, it's real! Slaughter has the entire set," said Virginia.

Junior removed the ring from his sister's finger and said, "If this is a real diamond, it will cut this mirror. If it's fake, then it won't cut the mirror." He took the ring and cut Mrs. Cottingham's hand mirror. "Virginia, you have a nice piece of diamond," Junior said, congratulating her.

Virginia went to her grandmother's bedroom where the rest of the family gathered. She shows everyone her present. Her mother's sister didn't seem pleased nor did her grandmother. They asked to see Slaughter. When Slaughter arrived in Virginia's grandmother's bedroom, the two women quizzed him about his intentions. Aunt Doris, a school teacher, mentioned Virginia's plans for college and Slaughter mentioned his plans to join the Army. Aunt Doris and Virginia's grandmother reluctantly gave their congratulations. Both, however, found it difficult to accept because of their ages. They knew they needed more education before getting married.

The couple left and went to Slaughter's brother's house. There, they sat in the living room and enjoyed a Christmas program on the television. Suddenly, Slaughter asked Virginia to step in the back, which she did, only to have Slaughter pull her into his niece's bedroom. Feeling uncomfortable, Virginia pulled away. Let's go back in the living room with your brother and his wife.

"Virginia, they know why we are back here."

"What do you mean? They don't mind us being here?"

"No, they don't. Besides I've already told my brother about my plans for the evening, and he said we could use this room."

"I feel uncomfortable with them being out there and we're in here."

Slaughter reached out and pulled Virginia close, touching and playing under her clothes. He made her feel excited and relaxed at the same time. Slaughter slowly placed Virginia's fine brown frame across the bed. Somehow, they undressed each other and started making love. Towards the end of their lovemaking session, Virginia experienced breathing problems. Slaughter removed his cock from her and took her to the nearest window. He hit her constantly in the back, trying to revive her.

"Are you alright Virginia? What's wrong with you?" Virginia struggled to catch her breath, finally saying that she's alright as she removed his hand from her back. "I just needed some fresh air."

"Slaughter there's something you need to know about me. I have asthma."

"Asthma? What's that?"

"It's nothing to be concerned about, it doesn't happen often. It causes me to have problems breathing. I'm alright now."

"Are you sure, Virginia?"

"I'm sure," Virginia said before kissing him tenderly.

Slaughter pulled away and told Virginia to get dressed. "I'm taking you home. I don't want anything to happen to you."

"I'm alright now. Promise me you won't say anything to my mother."

"Virginia, your mother has the right to know what happened."

"Believe me, if you don't want anything to change in our relationship, you will kept quiet about this. Unless you're prepared to tell my mother all the details, you handle the situation."

They dressed and returned to living room, and Slaughter never did agree to keep quiet about the asthma attack. Later, Slaughter took Virginia home. That night, he called to see how she was doing. Virginia assured him again that she was fine. A few moments after her conversation with Slaughter ended, Teddy called.

"Merry Christmas," said Teddy.

"Merry Christmas to you too. Why are you calling me? Especially this late at night."

"Well, I called earlier, but you weren't at home. Didn't your sister tell you?"

"No. Besides, she's asleep."

"How was your Christmas, Virginia? What did Slaughter get you?"

"What I got wouldn't interest you!"

"Come on. Try me! Tell me what he got you. Besides, I bet he couldn't beat my gifts anyway."

"I'm glad to say that he did."

"What did that scum get you?"

"He gave me an engagement ring."

There was total silence for a moment; then Teddy asked her to repeat what she said.

"You heard right. An engagement ring, and I'm looking at it right now."

Come on. You are joking with me, baby. Man, I don't believe this."

"What's the matter? The cat has your tongue? You didn't think that we were serious."

"Virginia, you can't go through with this. It will never happen. Do you hear me? Never." Teddy angrily hung up the phone.

Virginia smiled as she hung up the receiver. Thinking, I guess that takes care of Teddy...or does it?

A couple of days after Christmas, Teddy visited Virginia. Mrs. Cottingham spotted Teddy's car as she looked out of her bedroom window.

"Virginia, honey. It's Teddy!" she yelled. "He has just pulled up out there in the driveway."

"Oh, my God, it is Teddy! Mama, what am I going to do?"

"Child, I don't know what you are going to do. But you better think fast."

"Well, I guess I'm going to have to let him in," said Virginia as she left her mother's bedroom and rushed to the living room door. Virginia, visibly shaken, opened the door.

"What are you doing here?"

"Aren't you going to say hello and invite me in?"

"No. I shouldn't invite you in."

"But you will," said Teddy. "Hi Mrs. Cottingham, how are you doing?" He walked into their house.

"Fine. It has been a long time since we've seen one another. How do you like that college you're going to?" asked Mrs. Cottingham.

"I like it. I can't wait until Virginia graduates and join me," Teddy said as he looked at Virginia. Mrs. Cottingham left, leaving them alone in the living room.

"What are you doing here again?" asked Virginia.

"Girl, relax. You asked that earlier. I'm here to see you," he said as he pulled her close to him.

"You have no business here. I'm engaged!" said Virginia.

"What did I tell you on the phone?" Teddy said. "I meant what I said." He surprised her with a kiss on the lips.

"Now wait a moment, Teddy. You and I are over," said Virginia as she pulled away from him.

Teddy grabbed Virginia and said, "We are never over! Girl, don't you know that I love you and I always will? We have a history together, you and Slaughter have only months."

"No, we don't just have months together. Slaughter and I have established much more than simply a relationship. We have made an everlasting commitment."

Teddy looked deep into Virginia eyes and said, "Are you telling me that you and him have..." he tried, but he couldn't allow himself to finish the statement. He could see in Virginia eyes that she was no longer a virgin. He knew that she had slept with Slaughter. Something they never did.

Still, that didn't matter. He embraced her, saying, "Virginia, I still want you. Why do you think I didn't pressure you into having sex with me? I loved you too much to hurt you. I wanted you to be sure it was what you wanted." He reached for her hand and saw the engagement ring.

"So this is the big rock? Virginia, come let's go for a ride, some place quiet where we can talk." He grabbed and embraced her, kissing her all over her pretty brown face. "Baby, I love you a lot. Please tell me that you still love me." Virginia, surprisingly, responded to Teddy's kisses by not pulling away.

"You see? You still have feelings for me," said Teddy. "You and I just went through some hard times. Baby, I swear that's over. I'll never hurt you again. Here's forty dollars, I want you to have it."

"I can't take your money. Yes you can. I want you to have it. I worked at Eddies' so that I could have some money to take you out."

"You did that for me?"

"Yes, I did, I love you, Virginia. I'll do anything for you and anything to win you back. I'm leaving next week, but, Baby, I need to be with you. I just want to spend some time with you. Then if you still feel the same about Slaughter, I'll just have to accept it." He started kissing Virginia again when suddenly, her sister came in and said that Slaughter had pulled up in the driveway. Virginia quickly broke away, telling Teddy that she was sorry, but that he had to go.

"I'm not scared of Slaughter!" said Teddy.

Mrs. Cottingham came into the living room and asked Teddy to leave out the backdoor. Teddy refused. "Slaughter has already seen my car. Besides, I'm not afraid of him!" He walked towards the living room door to leave. Slaughter was already on the porch when Teddy walked out the door. They met face to face.

"Hey, man what's up? You don't have any business being here anymore," Slaughter said.

Rolling his eyes and patting his big Afro, Teddy yelled, "Oh yeah?"

"That's right, man. Like I said, you don't belong here."

"We'll just see about that! If that's so, why don't we meet at the bowling alley later, and see who belongs where?"

"Hey, man, you just name the time."

"How about an hour from now?"

"I'll be there," Slaughter said as he walked with Teddy to his car.

Teddy angrily got into his car and drove off. Slaughter walked over towards Virginia, who was standing on the porch. Slaughter kissed her and said, "What was he doing here?"

"I don't know," said Virginia. "I did not invite him here."

They went into the house and sat on the living room sofa. Slaughter continued to question her about Teddy. Virginia told him everything that happened except the kissing.

"Well, we'll just see about him refusing to leave you alone."

Virginia pleaded with Slaughter not to go to the bowling alley, Reassuring him that Teddy will get over her. It's you I love, not Teddy.

"I know you love me, Baby, but I'm just going over to the bowling alley to shoot some pool." Virginia pulled Slaughter to her, kissed him, and begged him not to get into a fight with Teddy.

"Are you sure that's all that happened?"

"Yes," said Virginia, who made him promise not to fight Teddy. Slaughter then left to go to the bowling alley. Virginia waited patiently, wondering what was going on at the bowling alley. Unable to wait any longer, she called Slaughter's house. Surprisingly, he answered the phone. "Oh, thank God, you are home. Tell me, what happen at the bowling alley? I've been worrying myself to death about you."

"Nothing happened," said Slaughter.

"What do you mean, nothing happened? Didn't you all talk?," asked Virginia.

"Yes, we talked, and I told him that he didn't have any business at your house. Then we played a game of pool. Didn't I tell you I wasn't going to fight him?"

"You mean you didn't pull out your razor?"

"No, I didn't. What did I promise you?"

"I know you promised me that you wouldn't fight. You were angry when you left here".

"Let's don't talk about Teddy anymore. Let's talk about how much I love you, and how I can't wait until you become Mrs. Slaughter."

I can't wait either, thought Virginia lovingly.

TROUBLE IN PARADISE

It's basketball season at Northeast High School. Virginia is working hard to prepare for the season. Northeast has had a victorious season leading their conference with a seven-to-two record. Southwest, their chief rival, had a seven-to-one record.

"Girl, it looks like we're going to make the tournament," said Virginia. "Mrs. Johnson said that she must speak with Coach Wheatland to arrange the hotel accommodations."

"Boy, I can't wait," said Rose. "Neither can I," echoed Virginia.

"Have you told Slaughter you're going away for a week?"

"No, I haven't discussed this with Slaughter. I shouldn't have to discuss this with Slaughter. He knew I was a cheerleader when we started dating."

"Did I hear you right? Have you forgotten that you must consider his feelings? You should discuss this with him."

"You're right. I'll discuss this as soon as I have more information about the trip. Slaughter is very understanding."

"Virginia, who do you thinks you're kidding? Honey, I see the jealousy in Slaughter's eyes when anything or anyone interferes with the time y'all spend together."

"Rose, why are you making a big issue out of this? Let's drop it, okay?"

Northeast and Southwest had a big game scheduled at the Macon Coliseum that night. The Pep Rally was a knock out. The cheerleaders were outstanding. Their routines lifted the spirits of the students. Guys swarmed around the cheerleaders after the game to help them take down their posters. Slaughter and Chiles, Rose's new boyfriend, looked on from a distance at their women.

The crowd thinned out, and Slaughter startled Virginia, approaching her from the rear.

"You scared me, Slaughter," she said.

"What's up, Virginia? I'll picked you up at the dance after the game tonight."

"That'll be fine," Virginia said.

"Slaughter, why don't you stop and bring Chiles with you?" said Rose.

"I don't keep Chiles in my wallet, Rose. However, if he needs a ride, have him contact me," he said before kissing Virginia and walking away.

The night was young and there's a big crowd at the Coliseum for the game of the season between Northeast and Southwest. Rose, Virginia, Carrie, and Stacy lined up with the others to cheer. The score was tied at halftime. Rose and Virginia took a break before their performance. Rose was going to get a coke when she saw Slaughter sitting in the upper deck with another woman. She looked again to make sure, and, yep, it was Slaughter. Still presuming that she was mistaken, she went to get closer to get a clear view. But it really was Slaughter with another girl.

Rose saw Virginia and distracted her so that she wouldn't see Slaughter. Before they performed another set, Rose asked Virginia if Slaughter had said he was coming to the game.

"Now, Rose, you know Slaughter is working, and that he doesn't like coming to games. He hates being in a crowd."

"Are you sure he didn't mention anything to you about coming to the game tonight?"

"No, he didn't. Now, let's hurry before we're late. You know I don't want Mrs. Johnson to make us run laps."

The cheerleaders performed at halftime. As Virginia was getting ready to do her gymnastic feat on the trampoline, she spotted Slaughter in the crowd sitting with another woman. Virginia was so shocked she hurt herself bouncing off the trampoline, onto the floor, in a split. She bravely completed the cheer, though she was in pain. Rose could see that Virginia was hurting. Once they finished their routine and had return to the sideline, Rose and Stacy helped Virginia who hopped on one leg to the ladies room. The girls got a closer look at Slaughter and the woman on their way there. Virginia glanced at them angrily as she passed in front of them.

"Virginia, are you alright?" the girls asked.

"Yes, I'm alright. I just pulled a muscle."

"Maybe you should sit down, I'll run and tell Mrs. Johnson what happened. I'm sure she'll understand," said Stacy.

"Oh, no, you don't. I'll be alright. I just won't do any more splits tonight. Besides, I need to keep moving this leg," said Virginia.

They returned to the floor and continued their cheers. Northeast led eighty-five to seventy-two.

"We're going to be winners tonight," shouted Stacy.

Virginia sadly hugged Stacy, agreeing with her. The crowd began counting as the game clock wound down. The cheerleaders rushed to congratulate their team and to greet their opponents to tell them what a good game they played. As Virginia hopped away, one of Southwest's players approached her. It was the team's star and lead player, Norman Green.

"Wait a minute," Norman said, reaching for her hand.

"That was some game you all played," said Virginia.

"What about us getting together after we leave here?" said Norman.

"Sure, I'll be at the school dance at Appling gym," said Virginia. "Okay, that's cool. I'll meet you there," said Norman.

Virginia left to get her pom-poms when Rose asked her if she was still going to the dance.

"Of course, I'm still going. I'm not going to let my leg stop me from enjoying myself. Besides, I'm supposed to meet someone there."

"Who?" asked Rose.

"You'll see," said Virginia with a smile.

They were headed for the exit door of the coliseum when Virginia and Rose spotted Slaughter. He chased Virginia and asked, "Aren't you going to ride with me?"

Virginia looked at his crazy eyes and said, "You got to be kidding. There is no way I'm riding in your car with another woman. You have made it obvious who you want to be with. You can kiss my blackass, Slaughter! I'll be damned if I'm going anywhere else with you again, do I make myself clear?"

Slaughter continued to chase her, saying, "This is not what you think, and please let me explain."

"You can go to hell and back before I let you explain anything to me anymore. It's over, Slaughter, do you hear me? It's over!"

Rose rescued Virginia and helped her to the car. "Leave her alone, Slaughter. This is not the time or place for you to explain what happened."

The two women got into Rose's car, passing Slaughter and his female friend along the way. In tears, Virginia glanced at Slaughter and continued to call him names.

"Calm down," said Rose. "I'm sure there's an explanation for this. Are you sure that Slaughter didn't say he was coming to the game?"

"Don't you think I would have told you? Would I be upset if he had told me?"

"Well, we're going to the dance tonight and have us some fun. I can't remember the last time I went to a dance with you. We always separate and go with the guys," said Rose. "Tell me

Virginia, who's the guy you're interested in?"

"Norman Green."

"How can you sit there all calm and say it's only Norman Green? Do you know how many girls dream of Norman Green asking them out?"

"Yeah. Who cares about Slaughter?" said Virginia.

"You do!" Rose said. "And you can't tell me you don't."

"Slaughter who?" she said, laughing off the pain she felt in her heart and leg.

They arrived at the dance and it's wall-to-wall people.

"Man, there are student from Southwest and Central here tonight," said Stacy.

"You're right," said Virginia, spotting Norman among the crowd. Norman also sees her and walked over. He asked if she wanted to dance.

"Of course, I would love to dance," said Virginia. They stayed on the floor dancing one record after another.

Rose watched as Slaughter entered the dance…alone. He approached Rose and asked, "Where is Virginia?"

"Virginia who?" said Rose. "An hour ago, you acted like you didn't know who Virginia was."

"Cut it out," said Slaughter. "Why don't you butt out and tell me where she's at?"

"Find her yourself, since you're the one looking for her!"

"Thanks a lot, Rose," Slaughter walked among the dancers on the dance floor, looking for Virginia. He finally spots her slow dancing with Norman. Slaughter got very angry, though he knew he caused this to happen. When the record stopped, Virginia and Norman left the dance floors and found a spot in a corner near the bleachers. As Norman was about to make his move on Virginia, Slaughter appeared directly behind him.

"Excuse me, can I have a word with you, Virginia?"

"I don't have anything to say to you, Slaughter."

"Is he bothering you, Virginia," Norman said.

"Oh, no, he's not bothering me at all. Let me see what he wants. When I return, we can finish our conversation," she said in her calmest voice.

"Okay, but don't take too long."

Slaughter grabbed Virginia by her hand and pulled her outside. They passed Rose and Chiles, who were snuggled up against the school building, kissing.

"What do you want?" said Virginia angrily.

"I want to talk to you and explain what happened."

"Oh, I know what happened. You aren't any better than Teddy!"

"No, you don't know what happened. And what do you mean comparing me with Teddy? You just assumed what happened by what you saw. What you saw isn't what it looks like. Besides, I saw a lot more at the dance. You and Norman were all hugged up together," said Slaughter.

"Well, you and that woman were all hugged up at the game."

"Look at me, Virginia, that woman means nothing to me. I wanted to go to the game and I didn't want to go alone. So I asked Alonzo's sister if she would go with me."

"Y'all carried on like you were more than friends. And why haven't I met this woman?"

"I don't know why I haven't introduced y'all."

"How would you feel if I went out with someone else?" she asked. "You wouldn't like it, yet you go and do this,"

"Virginia, lets go for a ride. Please," said Slaughter as they walked towards the car.

"No, I'm not going anywhere in your car."

Upon hearing this, he grabbed Virginia's arm and forced her inside the car. He explained to her what had happened as he drove. He decided to find a place to park so they could have a deep conversation. As soon as Slaughter parked, Virginia jumped out of the car.

"Don't you know that I love you?" he yelled.

"Love hell! You don't know the meaning of love. It doesn't mean being with me one moment and curled up with someone else the next," said Virginia. "Here's your ring back. Give it to that bitch since you have so much in common. Both of you hate crowds and hate being alone in a crowd. So give this to the bitch." Virginia tossed the ring in his car and walked off. Slaughter pleaded with Virginia to get back in the car. Virginia honored Slaughter's request. He drove off and took Virginia home.

The next day, the Northeast basketball team and cheerleaders were off to the sub-regional tournament in Augusta, Georgia. Meanwhile, Slaughter and Chiles had plans of their own to surprise the girls by attending the game. Slaughter and Chiles arrived in Augusta, registering at the Ramada Inn in room 227, next door to the girl's room. After the game, everyone returned to the hotel, excited over Northeast winnings, when the girls spotted Slaughter and Chiles in the lobby. Rose and Chiles greeted each other with a kiss and raced for their room. Slaughter and Virginia remained in the lobby to discuss what happen last night with Alonzo's sister. Slaughter grabbed Virginia, pleading for her to come with him to his room. He grabbed Virginia's ring finger and slips the ring back onto her hand.

"Slaughter, where do you think Rose and Chiles have gone?" asked Virginia.

"Don't worry about them, they're going to be doing the same thing. That's if they aren't already doing it."

The moment Slaughter commented about Rose and Chiles, Virginia heard them moaning and groaning something terrible. They were really into it. The music their bodies were making only increased the flame burning in her. Completely naked, Slaughter and Virginia forgot about the other couple and began making some body harmony of their own. So serious that Slaughter's rubber began irritating Virginia's, insides. She pleaded with Slaughter to remove the condom. Slaughter reluctantly stopped stroking her and removed the rubber. Then they continued their intense sexual escapade.

Afterward, they showered in the bathroom and continued their erotic adventures. They couldn't get enough of each other. Both sex drives were in high gear. They went back into the room and dressed in the dark. The girls told the guys good-bye and headed back to their rooms. Once there, Virginia called Slaughter to let him know they got there alright. Slaughter said that he would be waiting for her at school when they arrived tomorrow.

The next day, the buses were loaded and ready to leave for Macon. The players and the cheerleaders were in good spirits. Rose, Virginia, and some others were tired from their long night. Back at the school, Slaughter and Chiles waited patiently for the bus to arrive. Regina called out to them. "You must have been speeding Slaughter to beat us back."

"They left right after the game last night," said Rose.

"Sure, they did," said Regina.

"Who cares what she says? We are back now," said Virginia.

Slaughter dropped Chiles and Rose at Chiles' house, saying that he'll pick Rose up later. Virginia and Slaughter went to his house. His mother greeted them.

"I called your mother last night told her that my son went to Augusta," said Mrs. Slaughter.

"What did my mother say?" asked Virginia.

"She acted surprised, but she didn't get upset."

Slaughter changed clothes and left the house with Virginia to go to his brother's place. They spent some time with his brother and niece before he decided to take Virginia home. Mrs. Cottingham greeted them and told them about the conversation with Mrs. Slaughter.

"Slaughter, you're not going to let Virginia out of your eyesight too long, are you?"

"No. ma'am," Slaughter replied.

Mrs. Cottingham left Slaughter and Virginia alone in the room. She asked him about Rose. Slaughter said that he was going to pick Rose up at Chiles's house, and that Chiles was going to ride along when he took her home.

"You guys had this all planned, didn't you?" asked Virginia.

"Yes, we did," Slaughter said with a smile. "Well, Baby, I hate to go. But I got to pick Rose up and take her home."

"I know. I love you," said Virginia as she kissed her man good-bye.

A couple of weeks passed and the girls were getting ready to go to Atlanta for the basketball finals. Virginia, though feeling under the weather, still planned to go. This time, however, Slaughter couldn't make it because he had to work. A team remained in the tournament until a loss; one loss and you're out. They spent time together the day before she was to leave because he knew he couldn't see her the next day.

"I should tell your mother that you aren't feeling good so she can make you stay," said Slaughter.

"Don't do that. I'll only be gone for two days. I'll call you while I'm there."

In Atlanta, Virginia passed out while cheering on the floor. They rushed her off the floor. Mrs. Johnson decided not to let her cheer anymore. Northeast lost their first game and were eliminated from the tournament. Rose and Virginia called their loved ones when they returned to the hotel. Slaughter and Chiles were glad the team lost. Back in Macon, Rose told Slaughter that Virginia fainted during her cheers.

"I didn't faint," said Virginia. "I just passed out because I hadn't eaten anything. Anyway, the season is over and I can rest."

THE WEDDING

A month later, Slaughter received his notice about his entry date from Uncle Sam. Slaughter visited Virginia and told her the news. Virginia still didn't believe he was serious.

"I'm going in June 2," Slaughter said.

"That's right after graduation," said Virginia.

"That's right." Slaughter took Virginia to see his cousin, who recently had a baby. Gelinda, his cousin, asked them when they are going to set the wedding date.

"I don't know," said Virginia.

"What do you mean you don't know?" Gelinda asked. "It isn't everyday a girl gets engaged. Besides, aren't you joining the army, Slaughter?"

"Yep, I'm going to report on the 2nd of June."

"Girl, you better hurry up and set your wedding date. When are you going to finish basic training?" Gelinda asked Slaughter.

"We should finish in August," said Slaughter.

"That's a good time," said Gelinda.

"I don't want to wait until August to get married. I'd rather get married before he leaves, if we get married at all," said Virginia.

"It doesn't matter to me" said Slaughter. "But August would be fine."

A couple of weeks later, Slaughter got very ill. He had never felt this way before. He called Virginia and questioned her about her being pregnant. Virginia refused to believe that she could be pregnant. A month passed and Virginia doesn't have her period. She still, however, refused to believe that she was pregnant. Her mother noticed a change in her. Virginia finally told her mother about Slaughter's plans to join the army. Her mother advised that if she's going to marry him, to do it before he leaves. Or, if she waits, to consider going to college first. Virginia decided to get married in May—a month before Slaughter scheduled to leave.

She called Slaughter later that evening and discussed it with him. They agreed upon a May wedding. They informed family members and started making wedding plans. May was approaching, that means wedding bells for Slaughter and Virginia. Slaughter was becoming even more nervous as the big day neared. Virginia felt tired as the day got closer. She finally admitted to herself that she was probably pregnant. She arranged for her grandfather, who was a minister, to marry them. She asked Ellie to be her matron of honor. Rose felt hurt over Virginia's decision. Virginia chose Ellie for reasons she cannot discuss with Rose.

Right before Virginia and Slaughter had gotten serious, Ellie and Slaughter had something going on. Ellie was unaware that Virginia knew that she was trying to come between Slaughter and their relationship. Virginia asked Slaughter about the women in his pass, and he mentioned Ellie, but said that nothing ever happened. This was her way of knowing the truth about Ellie and Slaughter's friendship. She felt if Ellie's word could be trusted, then maybe nothing did happen, and Ellie wouldn't be a threat to their marriage. Seeing Slaughter and Ellie so close the following few weeks can only bring out their true feelings for each other and she can finally put the matter to rest. Virginia has to choose someone to give her away. Her mother suggested her uncle. However, Virginia's aunt Frannie visited them and encouraged her to pick her father to give her away. She explained to Virginia that she knows that her father hasn't been there for her and told her it was time to put their differences aside, especially on this day.

"I'll think it over," Virginia said.

Slaughter found out their parents have to give the court consent for them to marry. Virginia realized she has to tell her father about her wedding. Virginia and Slaughter went to see her father at his night job. There, Slaughter met Virginia's father for the first time and asked him for her hand in marriage. Mr. Cottingham, was reluctant at first, because of their ages. Slaughter tells Mr. Cottingham of his plans to join the army. Mr. Cottingham, however, was still not sure. He asked Virginia if there was another reason she wanted to get married.

"Dad, I love him a lot. We have been seeing each other for a while now and we're engaged."

"Virginia, look at me," said Mr. Cottingham. "Are you pregnant?"

"Dad, I could be," said Virginia, but that's not why we're getting married.

That convinced Mr. Cottingham to agree to give his permission to Slaughter to marry his daughter. Virginia asked her father if he will do her the honors and give her away at the wedding.

"Yes, I'll be glad to give you away," said Mr. Cottingham.

It's a practice day at the church, and everyone is present. Virginia noticed Slaughter and Ellie as they practiced in the premarital ceremony. Ellie doesn't seem bothered about the matter nor does Slaughter. Everything was going smoothly. Pop, Slaughter's best man, chatted with Ellie constantly. Virginia and Slaughter practiced coming down the aisles. Slaughter got cold feet but continued with the practice anyway.

"What's wrong?" Virginia asked.

"I'll be glad when this wedding is over," Slaughter said.

"Don't you want to marry me?"

"Yes, I do. That's a crazy question. I just know that a crowd of people will be here tomorrow, and you know how I feel about being around a crowd. But don't worry, Baby, it's going to be perfect." Slaughter placed his hand on Virginia's round, firm butt.

Everyone showed on the wedding day. Virginia waited in the chapel's classroom area, peaking out from time to time to see if she can see Slaughter's car. There was no sign of him. Aunt Frannie came in and found her outside the door.

"Child, what do you think you are doing?" said Aunt Frannie.

"I don't see Slaughter anywhere," said Virginia.

"He's probably running a little late. Everyone gets the jitters on this day, especially the groom. Don't worry. You're getting married," Aunt Frannie said.

Virginia walked over and looked out the window. She started thinking about Teddy, wondering if he had heard the news. Virginia also started questioning her feelings for Slaughter when her sister opened the door, saying, "Slaughter is here. We are ready to begin the wedding ceremony."

"Let's get started. Smile, Virginia!"

The wedding began with Virginia walking down the aisle with her father escorting her. After the groom kissed the bride, everyone gave their blessings, which brought tears of joy to the bride and the congregation. Aunt Frannie embraced Virginia, saying, "Everyone is crying because you all are so young. I will continue to pray that you have a happy and everlasting marriage."

Everyone left the chapel and went to Mrs. Slaughter's house for the reception. Everyone continued to wish their best for a successful marriage. Larry, a friend of Teddy's walked over to Virginia and said, "I didn't think this day would ever come."

"But it did, and I'm a very happy woman," beamed Virginia.

"I still believe if Teddy was here, this day would never be. Slaughter must feel very lucky today," said Larry as he placed a kiss upon Virginia's forehead.

Rose called out to Virginia and embraced her, saying, "It was a beautiful wedding."

"You aren't still mad at me?" said Virginia.

"No. Not as long as I know that I'm still your best friend, too," said Rose.

"You are more than anyone could ever dream to have as a best friend," said Virginia.

"Now, let's go and get you out of that dress."

While in the bedroom, Rose asked Virginia about their honeymoon.

We're not going to have a honeymoon, at least not like going away on a trip somewhere. I'm sure Slaughter is taking me somewhere special tonight; like a hotel." Virginia smiled.

"We graduate in two weeks, you know?" Rose said. "Are you going to march down those aisles as Mrs. Slaughter or as Miss Cottingham?"

"Girl, I'm marching as Ms. Cottingham. That's what I enrolled in school as and that's what I'll be graduating as."

The newlyweds left the reception and went to eat dinner.

"I can't eat another bite," Virginia said.

"You know you must feed our baby."

"I haven't taken the pregnancy test."

"You haven't had your period either, and I can feel that you are. This child is a girl. We are going to make an appointment with a doctor."

"I already have an appointment set for next week."

They arrived at the hotel and the desk clerk assigned them to room number 227. They embraced one another as they walked to their room. When they got to the room, and noticed the room number. They both said at the same time, "It's the same number we had at the Ramada Inn in Augusta."

"This must be our lucky number," Slaughter said as he picked Virginia up and carried her into the room. "You know this is a tradition." He placed her on the waterbed then made sweet love to her all night long.

Virginia's doctor confirmed that she was pregnant. The excited new couple told everyone the good news. Soon, they graduated from high school, and Slaughter started having mixed feelings about joining the army.

SLAUGHTER JOINS
THE ARMY

The day came for Slaughter to leave for Atlanta to take his physical examination, and from there to Fort Jackson, South Carolina for basic training. Virginia tearfully kissed Slaughter, squeezed him, and wished that he didn't have to go.

"My mother is going to take good care of you and our baby. I'm glad you decided to stay here with my mother. It's only going to be eight weeks then I'll be back home."

"I love you," Virginia said as Slaughter and his brother left for the bus station. She cried her heart out that day. It was easily the most difficult day in her life. She stayed in the bedroom with the door closed not wanting to see anyone. Slaughter's mother periodically checked on her, making sure she's alright.

Virginia received a letter from Slaughter telling her how much he misses her, mentioning the turmoil he's experiencing in basic training. It was the most challenging time in Slaughter's life. But having Virginia and the unborn child gave him the courage to meet the rigid training requirements. In basic training, Slaughter discovered one of the drill sergeants was running a scam operation. Knowing the trainees weren't allowed to have certain items, he allowed them to for hush money. The troops were ignorant of the procedures of legality pertaining to a sergeant and his troops. They drilled the troops constantly and punished them by making them pulled duties and extra duties. Slaughter had to pull KP-kitchen details duty. He hated it. He often dreamed and wished he were at home with his wife. Virginia's pregnancy was going well. Slaughter's brother took her to get a driver's license. She had grown tired of being dependent on someone to take her to places.

DECEPTIONS

Slaughter's brother Lucas was teaching Virginia how to drive. It was difficult because Slaughter's car is a stick shift. Shifting the gears and getting off the clutch at the right moment takes practice. One evening, Larry decided to pay Virginia a visit. Slaughter's sister Shelia is there. Larry and Shelia appeared to enjoy each other's company. Virginia, however, assumed that Larry's reason for coming over was to see Sheila. Larry mentioned a movie being filmed at the Central State Park featuring Billy Dee Williams, Richard Pryor, and other famous stars. The movie was *The Traveling All Stars.* They needed people to participate and paid twelve dollars a day. You had to sit in the baseball stands and cheer the team on.

"Virginia, you ought to try that. It'll give you something to do," said Larry.

"I'll think it over."

Virginia's mother confirmed what Larry said.

"Your grandfather is working there," said Mrs. Cottingham.

She called her grandfather, and he told her they still needed people. She told him that she wouldn't mind working there. Her grandfather thought it was a wonderful idea. He offered to drive her there. He picked her up, and they drove to the park. She was hired as an extra. The next day, she dressed for the scene in the dressing area. Virginia saw her cousin Debra among the crowd at the stadium. She spotted Teddy. Luckily for her, he didn't see her.

After they filmed the scene, Virginia returned to the dressing area, she changed and walked to her grandfather's car where Teddy, who was walking over to the car, spots her. Nervously, she exhorts her grandfather. "Start the car! I'm ready to leave!"

Noticing the unusual behavior of his granddaughter, he asked, "Are you okay?"

"I'm fine. I'm just tired," said Virginia. He then pulled off.

When she returned home, she decided not to go back. She feared seeing Teddy again and that he would cause trouble. That was the last time Virginia laid her eyes upon Teddy. Larry continued to visit Virginia. He sometimes would drop by pretending to visit Sheila, unaware Shelia was seeing someone else.

Slaughter wrote to Virginia and mentioned his graduation schedule and said he wanted her to be there. Virginia's doctors, however, vetoed any traveling, saying her pregnancy was too advanced for her to travel that far. Virginia cried when Slaughter called to find out what the doctor had said. And, although he assured her he understood, Slaughter silently accepted the news with much pain. He had looked forward to sharing his graduation day with his wife.

The day finally arrived that Slaughter came home from basic training. Virginia was showering when Slaughter entered the bathroom. Virginia pulled the shower curtain back and was startled by Slaughter. They looked at one another observing the changes in their appearances.

"I didn't realize you had gotten this big," said Slaughter.

"You have lost so much weight, and your complexion is darker," Virginia said then she kissed and hugged Slaughter. Slaughter watched her dressed, and then they went to the living room. There, they saw that Slaughter's brother Lucas and his family had stopped by. Slaughter and Virginia soon left the room and headed for the bedroom where they spent time catching up on the happenings. Virginia mentioned that Larry had visited her. She told Slaughter she thought he had an interest in Sheila. Larry didn't stop visiting Virginia now that Slaughter was back. Shelia, however, has developed a serious relationship with someone else. Slaughter was off again to his AIT School where he was preparing for training on administration. He chose administration to keep from being placed on the frontline if a war occurred. Slaughter wouldn't be away for long stretches anymore, and he can come home on weekends. His cousins are having a party. He wants to attend, but fear that Virginia may not want to go. He asked her, but she refused to go because of her pregnancy. She was having difficulty holding her water.

"I'll only be going back and forth to the bathroom. Besides, you wouldn't have fun with me there," said Virginia.

"What do you mean I won't have fun?" said Slaughter.

"You'll worry about me. Go ahead without me. Have fun. I'll be waiting for you when you get back." Virginia said all this, hoping that Slaughter would change his mind and stay home with her.

Slaughter didn't change his mind. To further hurt her, he put on the outfit Virginia had bought him. He kissed her and left for the party. Virginia curled underneath the covers on her bed alone. Slaughter was having a good time at the party talking with friends and relatives. His relatives boasted to everyone he was in the army. He was drinking heavily and smoking marijuana. Noticing an attractive girl seated at the kitchen table, he went over and sat next to her. Rapping' hard, he managed to get the young lady's attention.

"We've been sitting here conversatin', and you haven't even told me your name," said the mini-skirted lady.

"That's right I've haven't. By the way, the name is Slaughter, and yours?"

"Judy," She told him she attended Paine College in Augusta, Georgia. Slaughter asked her for a dance. There's a slow jam on, and Slaughter embraced her tight, causing her thigh-high skirt to rise higher. Later, he offered her a ride home. She accepted the offer. When they got to her house, she invited him in. No one was at home. They started kissing, which led to sex. Afterward, Slaughter tells her he's a married man. She said she already knew because she spotted his wedding band. "Too bad, y'all married," she said.

"But that still doesn't mean you and I can't keep in touch," said Slaughter. He gave Judy his address before leaving for home. It was late, and he knew she would be mad. She hadn't expected him to stay out this long. He hadn't expected to stay out this long either. He quietly entered the house, showered, and got into bed.

"Did you have a good time?" said Virginia, smelling the alcohol from his breath.

"The party was okay, I'm late because I took Ed home," said Slaughter, lying through his teeth.

The next day, Slaughter left for school. Virginia was getting bigger every day and feeling more miserable by the moment. Larry continued to visit, finding her more alluring than ever. Still, he pretended to be interested in Shelia. Hoping soon, he could let Virginia know how he felt when the time is right. Shelia decided to get married. This is shocking news to Virginia. She thought Shelia was interested in Larry. She asked Shelia about her relationship with Larry. Sheila informed her there was nothing personal between her and Larry. "I'm marrying Curtis Mathis," said Shelia. Virginia wonders how Larry's going to take the news when he finds out that Shelia is getting married. To her surprise, Larry took the news well.

Slaughter started cutting down on his weekend visits. The bigger Virginia got, the less she saw of him. Instead, he visited the Paine College campus where Judy lived and went to school. He told Virginia his feelings in his letters. He told her he was impatient waiting for the birth of their baby. The last time Slaughter came home, he accused Virginia of not getting enough exercise. They had a big fight, and Virginia was packing to go live at her mother's. Mrs. Slaughter overheard them arguing and intervened. She told her son the baby is going to come when it's ready.

"There's nothing you and Virginia can do to rush it," said Mrs. Slaughter.

"But, Mom! She has passed her date. I just want my wife to be with me." Slaughter went in the bedroom and pleaded with Virginia not to go. She continued packing, convinced that their marriage was over. Slaughter said, "If you're going to leave, then I'll take you home."

"No, I've already arranged for someone to pick me up," said Virginia.

"I brought you here, and I'll take you back if that's what you want."

"Isn't that what you want? I can't help it if this baby won't come. Maybe it's stuck!"

Slaughter reaches out to her, comforted her with a kiss and told her he loves her.

They decided that they were going to hang in there. The weekend ended.

Slaughter left and said, "You better be done had that baby with a smile." But Virginia took him seriously.

THE BIRTH

Rose called Virginia to talk, and Virginia explained how her life had been going. Rose encouraged her to get out of the house for a while. Rose said she was coming over and they could go to the mall. Mrs. Slaughter was relieved to see her daughter-in-law when the two friends returned from window shopping at the mall. She had called everyone looking for her. She called Virginia's mother to see if she had stopped there after work.

"When Mrs. Cottingham said you weren't there, and she hadn't heard from you, I assumed you were in the hospital."

"No, I haven't had the baby. Though I wish it was true what you were thinking," said Virginia. Rose mentioned to Mrs. Slaughter that Virginia was experiencing some pain.

"Virginia, are you feeling okay?" asked Mrs. Slaughter.

"Other than a mild pain, I'm fine. I just over did it today." Virginia had trouble sleeping that night. A sharp pain hit her in the stomach. She rolled over on the side of the bed and sat up. When she lied down again, another sharp pain hit her. Ow! She screamed at the top of her lungs, gripping the sheets on her bed saying, "It's time." The pain started coming in regular intervals. Mrs. Slaughter heard the scream and rushed to her bedroom, exhorting to her that everything was going to be alright. She telephoned Virginia's grandfather to take them to the doctor. She had to use the toilet, but Mrs. Slaughter encouraged her to hold off using the toilet, fearing her water would break. Virginia's grandfather arrived, nervous as hell. Going to the doctor, he drove along the curbside of the road, regularly checking his granddaughter's condition.

As the doctor attended Virginia, she cried out constantly for her husband. The nurse, thinking he was in the hospital, had him paged. She found out later he was in school at Fort Lee. The nurse stayed close to Virginia's side, comforting and holding her hands, while monitoring her situation. The doctor found difficulty in Virginia's labor and decided to give her a C-section. Still in pain, Virginia asked questions about the surgery.

"How big will the incision be?" she asked. "Why can't I have my baby naturally?"

"No, we must do a C-section and soon," said Dr. Grossman, who showed Virginia the small scar that remained on her stomach after her own successful operation a few years ago.

Slaughter had finished school and was driving home while Virginia was giving birth to their baby girl and still felt pain from the operation.

"Have you seen the baby?" she asked.

"Yes, and it's a girl. And, she's pretty like her mother."

"How did you get in here this time of night?" asked Virginia.

"I told them I was your husband. They already knew I was in the military."

"They wouldn't let anyone see me while they were prepping me for surgery. That's why I'm wondering how you got in."

"Do you want me to stay?"

"I wish you could stay, but they won't let you stay overnight."

Slaughter then kissed Virginia and left the hospital a proud papa.

The following day, the hospital okayed the release of Virginia and the baby. Slaughter, pick them up and brought them to his mother's house. As everyone prepared for Sheila's wedding and the arrival of the baby, excitement was everywhere. Larry brought the baby a gift, relishing the opportunity to see Virginia.

"Your mother decorated the house nice for Thanksgiving," he said to Sheila. "I have a gift for Virginia and the baby. The fruit basket is for Virginia and the present is for the baby."

"They're in the bedroom," said Sheila. Larry gave Virginia and the baby their gifts, complementing Virginia on how well she looked. In the kitchen, Aunt Lacey was telling anyone who would listen how lucky Slaughter was to have such a pretty wife and daughter. In her bedroom, Sheila overheard Larry's conversation with Virginia and wondered if he had an interest in her—or if he was only pretending to be interested. She told her brother what she thought. After receiving the tip, Slaughter started paying more attention to Larry's behavior around Virginia.

Larry stayed close to Virginia at Sheila's wedding reception. He said while admiring her outfit, "You sure don't look like you just had a baby."

"What do you mean I don't look like I've just had a baby? How is a woman supposed to look after having a baby?" she asked.

"Nothing. I just can't help noticing how radiant you look this evening." Slaughter noticed the attention Larry gave his wife. He walked over and pulled her away from him. "I'm ready to go," he said.

"Yeah, we should go and get the baby before she runs mama crazy," said Virginia. That night, Slaughter questioned Virginia about Larry always hanging around her. She admitted that it's strange, but they are just friends, "Besides, I'm married and very much in love with you," she said. He immediately dropped the conversation and started kissing Virginia, wanting to make love to her.

"Quit! We must wait until I have my six-week checkup. That way, I'll have some birth control pills," said Virginia.

"You didn't have the baby through your 'cutty cat.' Besides, I got some rubbers." He started rubbing and feeling on Virginia so passionately that she couldn't say no. Slaughter took Virginia and the baby with him when he left for Fort Campbell, Kentucky. Their mother's thought they're deciding in haste. So she asked them to speak with Virginia's doctor first. The doctor okayed the travel for Virginia and the baby, provided she see a physician at Fort Campbell. They decided to leave their baby. They returned a couple of months later to get their baby. Surprised at how much the baby had grown in such a short time. While there, Sheila told Slaughter that Larry dropped by and asked when they were coming home. Virginia looked on, hearing their conversation while feeding the baby.

LIES UNCOVERED

In Kentucky, Slaughter pulled a lot of duty. When not working, he hanged with the fells. Once, he had to pull duty in this large motor pool. The sergeant of the guards dropped him off at the motor pool, and he didn't even give him a weapon to protect himself from intruders. When he came home that morning, he told Virginia that he had never been so scared in his life. Receiving only the salary of a private, Slaughter had to hustle to make extra money for the family. So he repaired cars and gave rides in his car. Slaughter was notified to testify at a trail at Fort Jackson, SC. The army was bringing charges against the drill sergeant who took advantages of the troops when Slaughter was in basic training.

One evening, Slaughter came home with a bottle of gin. He told Virginia that he was going next door to hang out with the fellows. Virginia, as always, stayed home with the baby. While cleaning out the bedroom trunk, she found at least a dozen letters that Judy had written Slaughter. Virginia read the letters. One mentioned the first time they met. Which Virginia remembered because she was pregnant and didn't accompany Slaughter to his cousin's party. The more she read, the angrier she became. She couldn't understand how stupid she'd been, believing her husband loved her and, all the time, he was having an affair Judy.

Virginia—her heart broken into a million pieces—ran to the bathroom. She reflected on how she had put her husband on a pedestal. Virginia continued to read the letters while using the toilet, getting angrier by the second. Thinking, *He's not worth the shit I'm shitting.*

Before flushing the toilet, she grabbed the commode plunger and stared in the toilet. She stuck the plunger in the toilet and stirred her shit. She removed the plunger and placed it on some paper in the living room. Slaughter said he had a headache when he came home, but that didn't stop Virginia from confronting him with the letters. She hit Slaughter with the shit-covered plunger and cursed him out at the same time. Slaughter couldn't believe what was happening. He fell to the floor from the impact of the assault.

Once he realized what was going on, he grabbed the plunger from his irate wife and said, "Woman, you're crazy! What are you talking about?" She threw the letters at him and ran to the bedroom. Slaughter stumbled to the floor with a handful of Judy's letters. He realized he should have thrown out the damn letters. Virginia stormed out the bedroom saying, "I want to go home and I'm taking Carlene with me." Slaughter tried to explain that it happened a long time ago. She reminded him that not only were they married but that she was pregnant with his child. "How could you do that to us?" she angrily asked.

Slaughter realized that Virginia was over the edge, and all he could do was to take her to the bus station in the morning. That night, Slaughter slept on the couch while Virginia packed her belongings. Later, she fell asleep across the bed. Virginia woke up early, only to find Slaughter still asleep. So she asked her neighbor, if he would take her to the bus station. He agreed to give her a ride. She went back home to get her baby and suitcase, and Slaughter was standing at the door with his shotgun. "I'll shoot Iris if he takes you and Carlene away! I bought you here and I will take you back!"

Realizing he was serious, Virginia went and told Iris that Slaughter will take them and thanked him anyway. When she returned, she told Slaughter that he didn't have to get violent. "I just want to go home." Putting the unloaded gun away, Slaughter said he was going to see if   he can get some leave time from work. Slaughter never intended to take them home. Instead, he pleaded with Virginia to give him another chance. Slaughter received word from home that Virginia's grandmother had died. Also, he had a new assignment in Germany. He decided not to tell Virginia the news since they were going home anyway. Meanwhile, Virginia and her friend Cheryl went shopping. Virginia, for some unknown reason, searched all over for a black outfit. She found a black dress she liked and brought it. Slaughter, Virginia, and Carlene left Kentucky for Georgia Twenty miles from home, Slaughter told his wife the sad news about her grandmother's death and the funeral scheduled for tomorrow. She started crying and told him to stop by her grandmother's house first. Arriving, she found her father with family and friends in tears. They buried her the next day.

After the funeral, Slaughter packed his bags and was ready to leave for Germany. Promising Virginia and Carlene that they would be able to join him soon.

FIRST OVERSEAS ASSIGNMENT

Virginia received a letter from Slaughter a month later, saying that he found a place for them to live. He enclosed plane tickets with the letter. On their departure day, she kissed her mother and the rest of her family good-bye. Mrs. Slaughter drove Virginia and Carlene to the airport. Months flew by but not fast enough. Virginia was homesick and Slaughter was in and out. Her girlfriend Priscilla is having marital problems. Military wives had to endure constant separations from their husbands. This allows infidelity to enter the marriage. The soldier could easily have a legitimate excuse for being away due to their twenty-four-hour job requirement. The mission first and the family last. Priscilla revealed to Virginia that she found a train ticket in her husband's pocket. She also said that they didn't have any food in their house to eat. She said that her husband, Wolf, spends the money to go to the wall and buy sex from German prostitutes. Virginia questioned her naive friend. "How do you know that he's sleeping around?"

"Well, we haven't screwed in some time, and I found a rubber in his wallet," said Priscilla.

Virginia encouraged her to seek help. "I can't believe that he's doing this. Sleeping around and not buying food, why didn't you come to me earlier? You and your son Tony can come to eat at my house. You got to report this to his company." Virginia then referred Priscilla to the army community service for help.

One night, Virginia and Carlene went to the storage area. While there, she sees Priscilla with a guy. Later, Virginia noticed that Hillary, another girlfriend, always babysat for Priscilla. Priscilla and Virginia became very close, and she admitted to Virginia that she's having an affair with a married man. Virginia chided Priscilla that having an affair was no solution to her problem. Priscilla cries, "I'm tired of being left alone!"

The next day, the guys go out to the field for a month of duty. Slaughter, dreading the assignment, told Virginia he's getting out of the army when his time was up. Alice, another girlfriend, invited Virginia to go to a club with her to keep from being bored. The girls had a good time and vowed to go out again soon. The following morning, Hillary came by the house in tears. She had found out that Priscilla and her husband, Roy, have been having an affair. Virginia was shocked. Unable to believe Roy would have an affair. "He's always home with you. At least that's what I thought," said Virginia.

"I wouldn't put nothing pass Roy or any man when it comes to another woman. Priscilla is always asking me to babysit and I do. Meanwhile, they're out somewhere fucking. Wolf is never at home. He has a German girlfriend," cries Hillary. Virginia tried to calm her down, but Hillary kept on talking about it, getting madder by the moment. She ran from Virginia's apartment to face Priscilla—woman to woman.

Virginia got dressed and went after Hillary to stop her. She was too late. Hillary and Priscilla had already fought. Hillary wrecked Priscilla's apartment and her face, too, which she scratched and bruised. Mrs. Connors, a white German female, was holding Hillary. Priscilla admitted to everyone present that she had slept with Roy. Mrs. Connors, smiling, said, "Hillary whipped her ass good, and she deserved some more. But I'm not going to let her get in anymore trouble."

Virginia convinced Hillary to come to her place and cool off. As she entered the elevator, Hillary said, "I should go and beat her ass some more." Mrs. Connors said, "Honey, believe me, you tore her ass up. You won't have to worry about her anymore."

A couple of weeks later, Mrs. Connors's husband came home from the field and found her in bed with another soldier. Virginia couldn't believe what she's hearing as Chris and Hillary told her the story. "It was Mrs. Connors who told Hillary about Roy and Priscilla," said Chris.

"Yeah, Girl. I was in shock when I heard it," said Hillary.

They said Mr. Connors broke Mrs. Connors's arm when he beat her for fucking another man in their bed. "The guy jumped off the balcony naked. Chris had to get his clothes, so he would have something to put on," said Hillary.

"Boy, the guys are going to have a lot to deal with this time," said Virginia. The guys, after thirty days, returned from the field and are hit with the news that occurred during their absence. Slaughter couldn't believe that Hillary and Roy were having marital problems. Ditto, for the Connors, but by her being German, he wasn't that surprised. Virginia gave a "coming home from the field" party and invited Hillary and Roy. "You didn't invite Priscilla and Wolf. I figured you wouldn't so I did. I'm friends with both of them. Besides, that is their problem. Roy and Wolf get along at work," said Slaughter.

The guests arrived. Roy and Wolf exchanged words, then Roy left with Hillary.

"I told you not to invite Priscilla and Wolf," said Virginia.

Priscilla at that very moment was flirting with some guy to make Wolf jealous. Virginia fixed a drink while Slaughter watched her from across the room. When the last of the party goers left, Slaughter asked Virginia, "When did you start drinking?"

"I've been drinking for some time. I just don't drink every day like you do!" she lashed out.

"I'm sorry if I said something wrong. I don't mind you drinking. I just didn't know you ever drank before."

"That's not all I do. I've tried hash and marijuana," she continued.

Slaughter couldn't believe the change in his wife. Slaughter changed his mind about getting out of the army. He decided to reenlist for three years. They assigned him to stateside duty at Fort Gordon in Augusta, Georgia.

STATESIDE ASSIGNMENT

Virginia had changed a lot. Everyone saw the change in her behavior. She had matured and was ready to handle any challenge that confronted her. Pregnant again for the first time in five years, she looked upon it as a setback. She was hoping to get a job, instead she's pregnant. Slaughter was happy about the baby, hoping for a son this time. It didn't matter to Virginia as long the baby was healthy. The bigger her belly got, the less she saw of Slaughter. Leaving his wife and child at home, he had checked out every club in Augusta. She became very upset with Slaughter's going and coming. One night, she was so irate that she tripped and failed down the stairs in their apartment.

Slaughter came home and found his wife stretched out on the floor. He grabbed Carlene and rushed Virginia to the hospital. Thankfully, there wasn't any harm done to her or the baby. The sight of Virginia lying on the floor had scared Slaughter to death. They released her from the hospital the next day. Virginia was relieved that nothing happen to the baby. She once again started having problems with her pregnancy. The doctors were concern about her swelling. They decided to examine her further and found that Virginia could never have any more children. They informed her of their diagnosis and suggested she have a tubule done immediately after the C-section. The doctor's news devastated Virginia. She told Slaughter who was against the procedure. But since he didn't want to get a vasectomy, he consented for her to have the operation because it would be life threatening if she became pregnant again. Virginia saw a change in her husband's behavior after the birth of their son. He became jealous of her going and coming. He called home frequently to see what she was doing.

Months later, he received papers to go to Okinawa, Japan. Again, Virginia and the kids stayed behind until Slaughter could find a place for them to live.

FAR EAST ASSIGNMENT

Slaughter sent Virginia the tickets, and she left to join her husband in Japan. When she arrived in Seattle, Washington, she had passport problems. There wasn't a visa stamp on her passport allowing her to enter Japan. She was stopped at the traveling booth by the attending clerk who escorted her to the airline manager's office. They accommodated her with a hotel room, and provided transportation for her from the hotel to the Japanese Embassy. This was done so she could obtain a visa. The airline paid all of the expenses. *God was on my side,* she thought. They finally resolved the issue, and she was on her way to Japan. Arriving in Tokyo, an airline official told her they had rescheduled her connecting flight. The airline company, again, accommodated them with a fabulous hotel room, transportation and all expenses paid. Thankfully, they resolved the problem the next day, and she was on her way to Okinawa.

Slaughter was happy to see his family again. Unfortunately, the Japanese "Stealer Boys" robbed their home shortly after they arrived. It was hot that night, and they had fans in the windows in the bedrooms. The stealer boys somehow drugged the family before entering. Luckily, .they were only after money and didn't harm anyone. They reported the theft and received a refund. Several military families got burglarized that same night. Slaughter was reluctant about Virginia getting her driver's license and made up excuses not to take her. That is, until one of his friends volunteered to take her. He then immediately found the time to take Virginia to get her license. Slaughter started hanging out with a guy he met at work who liked to party. It got so bad that Virginia and the children never spent any time with him. He wouldn't even come home from work anymore. Thursday night, which was ladies night at the club, and weekends were party days for Slaughter.

One night, he was dressing and getting ready to go to the club. "It's ladies night," he told Virginia. "I'm going out for a little while, I promise to be home early."

She pleaded with him not to go. But he was more determined than ever to go. Virginia was so hurt she cried herself to sleep. She woke up later that night and still no Slaughter. When he finally came home, he found his wife sitting in the dark staring at the ceiling. He called out to her but she didn't respond. He shook her and still no response. Scared, he half-dragged, half- carried her to the bathroom and placed a cold towel over her face. Finally, he slapped her real hard, causing Virginia to burst into tears. He held her, hugged her tightly, and said, "What have I done to you?"

Although she felt better the next day, she realized she would have to do something with her life. She was too dependent on her husband, and it could destroy her if she didn't do something about it. She decides to attend college to further her education. She read a brochure about the Command Sponsor Program and applied for a Pell grant at the Education Center. She kept her plans a secret from her husband until the approval of the grant. He accepted the information by laughing at her decision, teasing her about going back to school, hoping she would change her mind.

Virginia, however, was more determined than ever to prove that she could accomplish her goal. More education increased her chances of finding employment and decreases her fear of insecurity. She maintained an A average in her first college quarter. Her instructor in business management advised her to major in business management because of the potential she displayed.

She began meeting people. She met Dana in her accounting class. Dana, a spouse herself, was unsure of her goals. Independence wasn't all she feared. Dana was overweight, and felt her husband's lack of attention to her was weight related. She used to be in the army, but since her husband serve in the air force, it made assignments to the same location difficult. So after she gave birth to their child, she didn't reenlist in the army. It was then that she saw a different side of her husband.

He verbally abused her in front of their friends and said exactly what he felt about her *fatness* when he had had too much to drink. In a way, Dana was attractive. She had a sweet personality and a beautiful face. She knew she needed to lose weight but found it hard being a housewife. Jobs were scarce, and that she formerly served in the army didn't carry much weight. So she enrolled in college to earn the hours she needed to apply for a civil service job. This way, she would always be eligible to apply for government jobs, helpful because Slaughter planned to make a career out of the military.

Dana's information encouraged Virginia to continue towards her goal. Though going to school and taking care of the family wasn't easy, family was her top priority, school was not enough. She wanted to make her own money. Feeling she couldn't do both, she quit college and decided to work for a while. She found employment as a sales associate in women's clothing at Afees Exchange. The starting salary of $3.75 an hour left her virtually broke after she paid the baby sitter and gassed up the car. She barely had enough money to buy clothes for work, let alone to buy for the children. Since her working didn't improve the financial situation of the household, she decided to go back to college. At least Slaughter could look after the children at night while she attended classes.

However, Slaughter wasn't dependable. Sometimes, he wouldn't call or come home from work. So she arranged with a teenage girl to baby-sit for her when needed. Dana couldn't understand why Virginia's man stayed away from her so much. Virginia wasn't fat and she wasn't ugly, yet her husband stayed in the streets. At least, her husband was always home. Still, something was amiss in both marriages.

One evening during a break in class, Dana said, "Girl, you're too good for Slaughter. I don't see how you do it. You keep your house clean, cook, and stay home with your children. I don't do none of that, and I go and come when I please, and my husband is always home."

"You should be glad that he's home and not in the streets. I wished my husband wanted to be home with the kids and me like yours do."

"I like to go places sometimes, but George never wants to go anywhere. So that's why I go…and I have a boyfriend too. I need somebody to say sweet things to me, to show me passion, and to make love to me. I just don't get that from George."

The instructor informed the class that break was over.

"I enjoyed our conversation," said Virginia.

"I'll call you tomorrow and we can talk some more," said Dana.

When Dana called, she invited Virginia to a cookout. Virginia wasn't sure. Then Dana said, "Slaughter isn't going to be home, and the kids can come too."

Virginia moaned. "I don't have a way to get there."

"I'll come pick you up."

"Okay. I'll come."

Virginia was having a lot of fun at the cookout, so were the kids. Dana introduced Virginia to one of her best male friends.

"Clarence Clayton is my name. Dana always talked about you saying that she wanted me to meet you. She didn't tell me that you was so damn attractive," said Clarence.

Virginia blushed and said, "Thank you," appreciating the come-on comments from the six-foot, 190-pound hunk.

"Dana, you didn't tell me that he's a big teaser."

"Hey, I do tease, but I'm serious, and Dana knows that I says what's on my mind. I'm not playing women when I say that you have some pretty big eyes."

"Quit, Clayton, you're making my friend feel uncomfortable," said Dana.

"I meant what I said. Now, let's play some cards so I can beat the panties off you girls. I'm teasing," Clayton said as he flashed his sexy smile. While playing cards he asked Virginia of the whereabouts of her husband.

"He's probably at home from work now," said Virginia.

"Oh, he didn't know you was coming here?" asked Clayton.

"Stop being so nosey!" said Dana.

"I just wanted to know why a pretty lady like you was here by herself. Honey, does your husband know that us jarheads— that's what they call us marines— can care less if a woman's married. If you were my wife, Honey, I would never let you out of my sight."

"That's enough!" said Dana.

"She still didn't tell me where her husband is."

"He's at home."

"Now, are you sure he's home?" said Clayton. "Yes, I'm sure."

"Don't pay him any attention," said George. "He's always doing people like that.

"He did me the same way," said Tonya as she placed her hands on Virginia's shapely thigh. Dana noticed that Tonya hung around Virginia a lot that day. She hoped that Tonya wouldn't make a pass at Virginia like she did her. A week later, Tonya called Virginia asking if she would do her hair. Virginia said, "Yes, I'll do your hair. How about tomorrow?"

Later that evening, Dana called. Virginia mentioned that Tonya called and wanted her to do her hair. Dana then told Virginia that Tonya is a lesbian. Hearing this news shocked Virginia, she had eagerly agreed to do Tonya's hair. Now she didn't want to be alone with the dyke. "Why didn't you tell me Dana!?"

"Maybe she won't come on to you like she did me," said Dana.

"Well, I'm not going to give her a chance."

Tonya came over, surprised to see Dana there. Virginia started talking about lesbians, how she hates them, and what she would do if one approached her. Tonya became very uncomfortable with the topic. "How did we get on this subject?" asked Tonya. "We are all married and fucking every night."

"Sometimes, I get sore from fucking every night," said Dana.

"Let's talk about something else," said Tonya.

"Girl, you sure did upset Tonya. Girl, I ain't seen her that nervous since I've known her. She was surprised to see me. If I hadn't been there, she would have made her move on you. But you don't have to worry about her now."

"Didn't I tell her off?" said Virginia.

"We sure did, Girlfriend," said Dana, laughing. "Virginia you do need to start getting out. You can go to club with me sometimes. I go by myself. Like I told you, I have to get out to keep my sanity or I'll go crazy in this damn place, waiting for George to take me somewhere."

"I would go out, but I don't like going by myself. People get the wrong idea when a woman goes out, especially to clubs by herself."

"Look at it this way: If still single, you would do many things by yourself, including going to clubs. And if a man made a move on you, and you didn't like him, you would handle it. A man can only go as far as a woman let him."

"You have a point."

"So what are you going to do? Go out or stay at home? Besides, Slaughter might change."

"I doubt if that would happen, But you're right, I need to start getting out more and quit waiting for Slaughter. Who knows, I may go out this weekend instead of sitting here by myself," said Virginia.

Dana called Virginia that weekend to see if she was going out and didn't get an answer. So, she assumed she went out with Slaughter. She called again and Slaughter answered the phone. Dana asked to speak to Virginia. Slaughter said that he thought she was with her. Improvising quickly, Dana told Slaughter that she was probably on her way over and hung up. Virginia never showed up. Dana left home and went to the club. When she entered the disco, she saw Virginia on the floor dancing. Suddenly, Clayton walked up behind her and saw Virginia dancing. Tonya, seated at a table, called out to both of them to join her.

"What up, Girlfriend?" asked Dana.

"Nothing much, what bring you guys out tonight?" answered Tonya.

"Now, Tonya, you know I come out every weekend, and during the week, too. I should be asking you that," said Dana.

"I figured I'd ask you since I asked Virginia," said Tonya. "She's sitting here at this table, too!" said Dana.

"I know it. But she's dancing now," said Tonya. "We can see that!" said Clayton.

"She needs to get out sometime. I thought she was with you until she told me that she came here alone," said Tonya. "She's been having a lot of fun."

Virginia returned to the table, and, in unison, Dana and Clayton asked, "What has gotten in to you?"

"Nothing. I decided to take your suggestion and I feel damn good now."

"Where's your hubby?" said Clayton.

"Home with the children," Virginia said.

Dana asked Virginia to accompany her to the ladies room. While there, she told her that she had telephoned and Slaughter answered, thinking they were together.

"Well, I don't know why he'd assume that! He wasn't at home when I left! The kids are at the sitter's house," said Virginia. "He was trying to get me to say that I didn't know where you were. Anyway, I played him off, and he believed we're together," Dana said.

"I don't care what Slaughter thinks anymore. I'm going to do what makes me happy. I'm fed up waiting for him to come home. I'm going to have some fun too. Besides, he's always telling me he's going to the club."

"Let's go back to our table, Girl, and throw down tonight."

"There's going to be a party at this club tonight," Virginia said as they switched their bottoms back to their tables.

Slaughter remained at home waiting for Virginia and the children to come home. When they came home, he remained patiently in bed until she tucked the kids in, changed, showered herself, and joined him. Then he asked, "Where have you been?"

"Out!" she said. "Where?"

"To the club, that's where."

"Dana, called for you. Did she tell you?" he said assuming she went with Dana.

"Yeah, she told me."

Then Slaughter, as usual, got horny and wanted to go up in his wife.

To his surprise, Virginia declined the screw. "Woman, what's wrong?"

"I'm tired and I don't feel like fucking.

"You should have thought about that before you went out," Slaughter said before forcing himself on her.

Virginia now had the courage to go places and do a lot by herself. She went to parties, neighborhood cookouts, and occasionally to the club. She didn't go out as much as Dana, but she got out and enjoyed herself—and felt good about it. Slaughter continued to go out every chance he got.

Clayton and Dana became very close friends. He was engaged to a girl name Linda, who was jealous of his friendly relationship with Dana. Linda assumed there was more to the relationship. Clayton felt caught between the two. He valued Dana's friendship. He knew her before he became engaged to Linda. Linda was a schoolteacher and Clayton a marine, so they had 'difficulty associating with each other's friends. Virginia and Clayton also became friends. He needed another ear to listen to his problems with Linda. He also supported Virginia continuing her education. Clayton encouraged Dana and Virginia to believe in themselves.

One day, Clayton called Virginia to tell her that Dana was depressed over something George had done to her. So she paid her friend a visit. Clayton was wrong. Dana was depressed because she had broken up with her lover. Clayton didn't know Dana's boyfriend or he would have mentioned it to Virginia. She listened as Dana explained what happen. She was through with having a relationship, and she wanted to spend time home with her family. However, she also felt miserable. Already, she missed her married lover who was also a member of the air force.

Virginia gave support, saying, "You did right, that's the only way you can give your marriage a chance." Clayton called to check to see how Dana was doing. Then he asked to speak to Virginia. Virginia told him, "She's doing alright. now that I'm here."

That weekend, Slaughter tells Virginia that he's going to a company party. As usual, he doesn't invite Virginia. She doesn't feel well, but doesn't tell Slaughter because it wouldn't have made any difference. He would have gone anyway. That same evening, Clayton and Linda went to the club at Tori Station. It was Linda's girlfriend's birthday, and they decided to take her out. While there, Clayton saw Slaughter come in with a woman in his arm. He changed tables so he could be closer to Slaughter and the woman. Slaughter and the woman appeared more than friends.

He excused himself from the table and went to the lobby to call Dana to tell her what he was seeing. Normally, Clayton wouldn't do this. He told Dana, "Virginia is too good a woman to have to put up with scum like this."

"What do mean you wouldn't tell your friend if you saw her husband with another woman? You mean you wouldn't tell me if you saw George with someone else? I would never speak to you again."

"You know George isn't going anywhere, Dana. Listen, I have to go. I'll fill you in tomorrow about what happened. I just had to tell someone. It's making me sick, and I don't know how long I can stand it. I ought to go over and ask him about his wife."

"You stay out of it. Go back to your table and have fun with Linda."

Later that night, Dana received a call from Virginia, who was suffering a tremendous amount of pain. Dana rushed over. When Dana arrived, Virginia had dressed and asked Dana to take her to the emergency room. "I don't know what's going on with my body. I'm having stomach pains," said Virginia. At the hospital, they treated her for a urine infection and sent her home. On the way back to Virginia's house, Dana broke down and told Virginia about Slaughter being with another woman. Dana was upset. Her best friend was sick and her husband didn't give a damn. If he did, he wouldn't have been out with another woman, she angrily told Virginia.

Virginia asked, "Who did you hear this from? Who told you this!?"

She screamed. Dana pulled up in Virginia's driveway.

"Calm down, Virginia. I shouldn't have told you this, especially since you're sick."

"Forget about my being sick and tell me who told you this," said Virginia.

"Okay, Virginia, let's go inside and get you to bed then I'll tell you."

Once inside and in bed, Dana told Virginia that Clayton called and told her. She related to Virginia everything that Clayton said. She said that Clayton saw them walk in together and sit at a table alone. They danced and enjoyed each other's company. She told Dana to have Clayton call her tomorrow. Virginia got very angry that night. She doesn't cry over Slaughter this time. She stayed awake until he came home. Slaughter came upstairs and found Virginia and Carlene in bed. "Carlene, you can go and get in your bed now."

"But, Dad, I want to sleep in here with mom, 'cause she's sick, and Mrs. Dana told me to look after her."

"Virginia, are you?" asked Slaughter.

"Dad, mom's sick. Mrs. Dana had to take mom to the hospital 'cause you weren't here. Dad where were you?"

"Carlene, don't worry. You can go to bed now. Dad went to a company party." He then walked Carlene to her bedroom and put her in bed.

"So tell me, now that Carlene's in the bed, how was the party?" said Virginia.

"It was okay. But, Honey you didn't tell me you was sick."

"Would it have mattered?"

"Yes, it would have mattered. What did the doctor say was wrong?"

"It's nothing serious. I just have a urine infection. They gave me some medication for it."

"Let me see what they gave you," said a concerned Slaughter.

She didn't question Slaughter anymore that night. The next day, Clayton called Virginia and told the whole story. She asked him to describe the woman. "Why, do you think you know this woman?" he asked.

"Maybe, why don't you just tell me how she looks?"

Clayton described the woman over the phone. She thanked him, but Clayton didn't want thanks. He could tell from Virginia's voice that she was upset. Upsetting her was the last thing he wanted to do, especially since she was sick.

"Don't worry about me," Virginia assured him. "Say a prayer for Slaughter. He's the one who's going to need it." She called Slaughter at work, asking how his day was going in her sweetest and most loving voice. He asked how she was feeling and she said she was doing fine. Then she dropped the bomb. She asked for Carolyn's telephone number. Slaughter got silent for a moment, before asking, "Why do you want her number?"

"I thought I would call her. Maybe even drop by her place," Virginia said.

He said that he'll call back and give it to her because he didn't have it now. When they hung up, Slaughter called Carolyn and warned her that he think his wife knows they were together. Meanwhile, Virginia called Dana and asked her to come over. When she arrived, Virginia had dressed.

"Where do you think you're going?" Dana asked.

"I want you to take me to Tori Base."

"What's going on?"

"I know who the who is and I'm going to tell her black ass off." Dana knew she couldn't talk her girlfriend out of what she was about to do. So she drove her to the post. They went to Carolyn's barracks so they could talk. She admitted being with Slaughter, "It's not what you think!" she said.

"The hell with what I think! I hope he's more helpful to your mental, physical, and sexual needs. Believe me, I'm going to destroy you both. You can't endure an adultery case, especially since you're in the military, too. Plus, he has two children to provide for. You're definitely going to need a job. Didn't he tell you I'm giving him custody of the children?" she asked.

Not waiting for an answer, she continued to slander Carolyn until Dana said, "That's enough, Virginia, let's go."

When Virginia returned home, she threw Slaughter's clothes out the front door. The children looked on from a distance, not knowing what was up with their mother. Dana comforted the children, before sending them to their neighbor's house across the street. Meanwhile, Virginia continued to throw Slaughter's possessions out. Slaughter arrived and tried to explain to Virginia what happened.

"Get your stuff and get out! I'm sick of taking all this mess from you! All you do is use and hurt me! I don't give a damn about your career. I've had it! You're getting out and you can tell your bitch for me that she ain't heard the last of this!"

"Dana, talk to her," said Slaughter.

"I can't talk to Virginia. She's upset and rightly so," said Dana. Then Slaughter grabbed Virginia and said, "I'm not going anywhere. These are my quarters!"

"We'll see about that," said Virginia as she broke loose and ran next door to call the military police. Virginia made the call, returned home, and told Slaughter that she had called the MP. Slaughter laughed. "These are my quarters. I'm not going anywhere."

Virginia, still hurt, continued to throw his possessions out. While Slaughter paced the floor telling Dana, "I not going anywhere."

The MPs arrived and said they were to mediate a domestic dispute. Virginia quickly informed them that she called. She said they were having a domestic disagreement and that she wanted him out before they started fighting. The police, seeing the state of mind of Virginia, told Slaughter that he must leave the quarters. He whined, "I signed for these quarters!"

One of the military police quickly replied, "It's a privilege for you to have quarters. You are only authorized quarters because of your dependents. These are your dependents' quarters. When there's a domestic disagreement, the sponsor is removed from the quarters. They escorted Slaughter to the bedroom to get his personal items. When they returned from the bedroom, Slaughter asked when he could return. "In forty- eight hours," one of the MPs said. "But only if your wife agrees to it." Slaughter, hurt and angry, looked at Virginia. Virginia feeling the same way, looked back as they escorted him to his car. They escorted Slaughter to the barracks where he had to remain until the situation was settled. Meanwhile, Dana was shocked to learn that the quarters belonged to the dependents. She told Virginia, "Slaughter was feeling mighty shitty when they threw him out. Well, if you need anything, you just call me."

"I'll be alright now that he's out of here," said Virginia.

That night, Clayton called Virginia to see how she was doing. He had heard what had happened from Dana. He couldn't believe that Slaughter didn't know what would happen to him if there were a domestic problem in the home. Virginia, angry and hurt, didn't won't to talk about it. He understood and told her to call if she needed anything. She thanked him for calling and hung up.

Slaughter called, hoping his wife would let him come home. "I'm sorry for what I did," he said.

"You've gone too far this time," said Virginia.

"My commander has arranged for us to see a marriage counselor. They should be contacting you. Maybe that's what we need. I'll see anybody as long as I can come home."

Virginia relented and said he could come back home in forty-eight hours. A changed Slaughter returned home. Although he had agreed to get counseling, he still was angry with Virginia for putting him out. He suffered embarrassment because everyone at his company knew his wife had him kicked out of his quarters. He became so angry, that it made him drink more, especially when he had to see the counselor, who he hated. He didn't want to discuss his marital problems with anyone.

Virginia did all the talking at the sessions. He knew that the only way to get out of counseling was to give her what she wanted. So he started coming home and spending time with the family. One day, he called Virginia from work and told her their session was cancelled. Further, stating the counselor would contact them later to reschedule. Time passed, and she still hadn't heard from the counselor. So she call him and asked, "Why haven't he scheduled another session for us?" Dr. Krebbs said, "Your husband said everything was fine and counseling wasn't needed any more."

Virginia realized then that Slaughter didn't want help, and she changed from that moment on, treating Slaughter the same way he treated her. Slaughter saw the change in her. They started arguing and fighting frequently. Only this time, it was because he'd be angry after waiting for her to come home. She didn't come home promptly every night after her class. Sometimes, she'd be two or three hours late coming home.

Slaughter decided that his babysitting days were over. So Virginia either got a sitter or took the children to the Child Care Center. She was determined to finish school and to take some time to enjoy herself. Slaughter had no interest in being a family man, only a provider. She still found time for the kids and gave them plenty of love, advice, and stressed the importance of education to be successful.

One Saturday evening, Slaughter dressed and went out. Later that evening, Virginia dressed and went out too. She drove to the Kadena Air Force Base Club. She seated herself at a barstool and ordered a drink. At home, Slaughter had returned, only to fine Sandra, the baby sitter, there. He asked her, "Where did my wife say she was going? How long have she been gone?" Getting no answers from Sandra, he called Dana. He asked her if she had seen his wife. Dana said, "No, I haven't heard from Virginia." Slaughter, upset, left the house and went to the club to find his wife. Virginia still sat at the bar drinking and looking longingly at the dance floor. Some guy approached her and asked her to dance.

"No, not now, maybe later," replied Virginia.

Slaughter spotted his wife at the bar as soon as he had entered the club. He joined her. "I didn't know you wanted to go out tonight," he said.

Shaking her body to the music, Virginia said, "I know you didn't.

There's a lot you don't know about me. Are you surprised to see me here by myself? Well, it's time you learned. I've been going to the club by myself a lot. You see, I'm a single woman. Married on paper, single in reality. Shocked? Well, don't be because I'm your wife, the one you've created. I don't have no one to be home with. So when I get the need to get out, socialize, and have fun, I go alone,"

"Let's not argue. What are you drinking?" he asked. "Gin and orange juice."

"Do you want to move to a table?"

"You don't have to stay. I came alone and I can leave alone."

"No, we haven't been out together in a long time, and I'm having fun."

She could see from the expression on Slaughter's face that he wasn't having fun. Yet, they stayed there anyway. That night, Slaughter saw his wife in a different way. For the first time in a long time, he had to admit to himself that Virginia had changed. The girl he married would never go to a club by herself. The little teenager he married and manipulated had become a woman. A woman prepared to face the world. Scared, he knew if he didn't change his lifestyle he could lose his wife —that's if, he hadn't already.

Slaughter asked Virginia on her class night if she was coming straight home from class. She assured him that she was. She was in a studying, no nonsense mood, having less than a year to go before graduation. Clayton and Linda started having problems again. Problems that were so serious that they broke off their engagement. Slaughter became aware of the friendship between his wife and Clayton. He thought of the worst and Virginia let him think the worst. He came home and overhears her talking on the phone to someone. From the conversation, he knew it wasn't Dana. Clayton hearing Slaughter in the background says, "I wish you would let me be your man. I'll treat you better than he's doing any day of the week."

Virginia heard a click in the phone and knew right away that Slaughter is listening in on their conversation. So she told Clayton she has to go then hung up the phone. Hearing his wife laughing, Slaughter angrily asked, "Whom were you talking too?" She deliberately lies to see his reaction. "I was talking to Dana. Why?"

"I just wanted to know."

Virginia saw the jealousy written all over her husband's face. That evening, Virginia told Dana of Clayton's phones call and that he told her that he and Linda were breaking up. Dana said, "He called me and told me that Slaughter picked up on the other phone. I told Clayton that Slaughter was not like George and that he gets jealous at anything you do while he plays the field. Clayton said that he's going to invite himself to dinner at your house one day and really make Slaughter jealous. You know he will do it. He is always teasing us. He does me like that, but George knows how crazy he is, Slaughter doesn't. Slaughter will take him serious. Especially since he knows that he has messed up and that you know about it. He would feel that you like him," Dana said.

"Slaughter would think twice about that," said Virginia.

One evening, Clayton stopped by Dana's house. Still hurting over breaking up with Linda, and not wanting to cook, he invited himself to dinner. He then called Virginia to see what she was cooking and invited himself for dinner. Dana warned him not to go to Virginia's because Slaughter is very jealous, and he wouldn't want to cause trouble for her.

"I've already met Slaughter, and he invited me to come to his place anytime," said Clayton.

George tried to tell Clayton that Slaughter is crazy. "I don't know, Dana. The man said that he had met Slaughter. Anyway, like you and Clayton are friends, he is Virginia's friend. Man, go ahead and do what you want to," said George.

Clayton decided to go over to Virginia's. Dana called and warned her that Clayton was on his way over.

"It's alright if he comes over for dinner. I always cook plenty," said Virginia. By that time, her doorbell rang. It was Clayton and Slaughter welcomed him in. He talked during and after the meal, talking about women and how difficult they can be. The evening turned out good. Slaughter recognized Clayton's voice and realized he was the one Virginia was talking to the other day. He felt foolish now, thinking that his wife was having an affair.

Slaughter's stint in Japan was getting short. Clayton had already left for his new assignment that left Dana and Virginia feeling alone. The girls hated to see their friendly relationship with Clayton end. Virginia and Dana toured the far east. They went to the Philippines, staying at a hotel outside of Clark Air Force Base. Merchandise was very cheap, still, poverty was everywhere. The young Filipino prostitutes started hoeing as early as twelve to assist their families.

The soldiers assigned to the base were very vulnerable to these fast- loose women. Every club, including the post, had an almost-naked women dancer for entertainment. It was shocking to see the soldiers especially the married ones chase after those woman, treating them like gold. There were many married and single soldiers living and visiting the country and indulging in their sexual fantasies. Drug peddlers sold their poison in the streets at all hours. Selling "items" among the streets were plentiful. You could set your price to purchase any item you wanted. Wheeling and dealing was the way to shop in this country. We stayed in the Philippines for a week before leaving for home.

Virginia's children were glad to see their mother. They told her what they had done and what their dad didn't do. It was their first time they had been separated from their mother. They couldn't bear the thought of being without her. Virginia and Dana, however, had already decided to tour Korea. Virginia immediately informed the family of her plans. Slaughter reluctantly allowed her to go.

When they visited Osan Korea, they found the same environment. Poverty, prostitution, drugs, and wheeling and dealing to buy items. The Black market was plentiful. They were issuing a ration card worth seventy- five dollars to buy merchandise at the Post Exchange. They based the amount on their length in stay in the country. This time when they return home Virginia found her children had adjusted better to her absence. Slaughter complained about missing her. He now realized how he depended on her. Managing the household was a big job. He didn't want to even contemplate losing her, leaving him to do the job himself.

One day, Virginia noticed her babysitter, Sandra, clinging to Carlene's doll baby. Another day, she saw Sandra in the Post Exchange buying clothing for her cabbage patch doll. Virginia called Sandra to babysit for her. Sandra said, "I'm not babysitting anymore because I'm going back to the States. The news disturbed Virginia. Sandra had been good help for her family, especially while she traveled to the Philippines. She remembered Carlene saying that Sandra was mean to them when she babysat. Virginia, however, didn't pay Carlene any mind, believing her daughter made the story up so she would feel guilty about leaving them.

Virginia later found out from Sandra's sister that Sandra had gotten pregnant by a young marine and that was why she went back to the States. Virginia told Slaughter, who had to make sure he came home from work so he could look after the kids when Virginia was in class. They drew closer but still it wasn't the same. They had changed. He wanted to be near the family and the family was getting used to him being there.

Since Dana and Virginia couldn't hang out anymore. Slaughter filled the gap by spending more time with his family. Though she enjoyed Slaughter spending time at home, it became uncomfortable. The family became more aware of his heavy drinking. A month before the Slaughters left Okinawa, a typhoon hit the island. It had been a while since a tropical storm hit this island, and the weather bulletins predicated a bad one.

The Slaughters and Clara rushed out to do some quick shopping after hearing the bulletin, preparing themselves for the storm. The lines at the commissary seemed never ending. A news report announced that it could be the worst storm to ever hit Okinawa. The forecast predicted the storm to arrive in two or three days. When we returned from shopping, the wind and gust had become very strong. Slaughter checked to make sure that all the windows had typhoon tape on them. They strapped down the trashcans to keep the heavy winds from blowing them away.

Looking out their windows, the Slaughters saw trees, grass, and loose debris blowing throughout the neighborhood. Virginia recalled the first time she experienced a typhoon, living off post. That was the first time in her life she had been exposed to that type of fear. Locked in the house with shuttles closed and secured. To make sure they had drinking and washing water, they kept the bathtub, sinks, and washing machines filled with water. The roaring winds, trembling window shuttles and the continuous rainfall scared Virginia and the children to near death. Slaughter saw the glazed looks on his wife's face, grabbed her and said, "What were you thinking about?"

"I was just remembering when we experienced our first typhoon."

"Yeah, that was something else. But now we're living in quarters. They built these quarters to handle these storms. Honey, believe me we are safe. Concrete material is inside and outside. That's why they released all the soldiers who have families home to their quarters."

"I hope you're not saying that you are looking forward to this."

"No, but at least I don't have to go to work. Besides, we can go and get in the bed and make love. We got plenty of food, water, and beer."

"We had adjusted well to their culture and the tropical storms. The Japanese preserve water by a tank installed on the roof of their homes. So, if the typhoon season doesn't hit, they'll still have water during a water shortage, which could last for months. You would have water one day, then no water the next day, or it would be off and on sporadically during the day".

"We experienced this process during the year 1981. Those times were rough, but we made it through. Typhoons are a blessing for this far-east land, because they filled their reservoirs with water. Though the Pacific Ocean is near, its water can't be purified for drinking. Finally, the time for us to leave this land where we had so many wonderful experiences came."

SECOND STATESIDE ASSIGNMENT

The time came for them to leave Japan and return to the states. Their destination was Fort Dix, New Jersey. Slaughter had an accident a few months after their arrival. He had been drinking and lost control of the car, totaling it. Luckily, they didn't give him an alcohol test or he would have lost his driver license. From that day on, Slaughter made a vow to stop drinking, w hich he did for a while before going back on the wagon.

Virginia noticed that Slaughter was drinking more since he was home more. He would get violent and called her vile names. One night she said she was going out with the girls because she hadn't been out in a while. She got back late, the exotic male strip show they went to didn't end on time and Lillie wanted to stay at the disco. Thinking her husband wouldn't mind, Virginia agreed to stay. When she got home, to her surprise, Slaughter had double locked the door. So she knocked on the door until Carlene let her in. Slaughter had called her a whore and threw her nightgown at her. Virginia tried to defend herself, then realized it was hopeless. So she changed clothes and slept on the couch. Moments later, Slaughter came and dragged her off the couch, saying, "No wife of mine sleeps on the couch!" Then he forced her into bedroom. Virginia didn't want to sleep with him, especially since he had been drinking, so she pulled away. He pulled her back tearing her grown and throwing her to the floor. Virginia tried to break away before realizing that it was hopeless. She stopped defending herself and went with him to the bedroom. She told him that he hurt her and he offered a weak "I'm sorry."

Later on, he wants to make love and Virginia refuses. He wouldn't allow her to change gowns; the one she was wearing was all torn up. She might as well been naked. Slaughter turned off the light and forced himself upon his wife. He took her savagely, much to Virginia's delight. Months later, Virginia received a notice in the mail about her civil service rating. She passed. It was only a matter of time now before she would have a job. She told Slaughter the good news, which made him excited for his wife. He had some news to share too: He'd come down on levy for duty in Berlin, Germany. She couldn't believe this was happening. She had finally gotten the opportunity to get her career off the ground and this happens. She confided in her girlfriend Regina who told her that she had a good chance to get a job over in Germany.

Regina then told her about the murder that occurred at the Guest House involving a female soldier and her son. The soldier had gone to get him from a mental facility, hoping that he would be ready to join her at Ft. Dix. She said he had suffered a mental breakdown when he learned his mother had committed him to the mental hospital. While having the breakdown, he attacked his mother when she returned to their room from work. The receptionist in the lounge heard a loud noise upstairs. One of the clerks checked to see what was going on and discovered nothing. Meanwhile, the son had thrown his mother up against the wall, knocking her out cold. Then he took a butcher knife and cut her chest open, removing an internal part before spooning his mother's eyes out. The boy then ran to the receptionist area, all bloody, and tried to grab the clerk. Fortunately (due to the glass booth), he was unable to reach the clerk and kill again. Seeing the blood stains, the rage in his eyes, and the bloody butcher knife, the clerk immediately call the military police. He ran to his mother car, seeing he couldn't get to the clerk. The military police arrived, made their arrest and removed the body.

Regina was so disturbed by what happened that she quit her job. "Virginia I'm surprised you didn't hear about this," said Regina.

"Girl, Slaughter mentioned it to me. I was in the area when it happened. The police had roadblocks all along that street," said Virginia.

"Well, I'm glad you didn't go to the Guest House."

"Now that I've heard again what happened, I'm definitely not staying there."

After hanging up, Carlene gave her mother the mail. She received a letter from Hillary and Roy that contained some sad news. Hillary said that she had finally gotten pregnant, but she lost the child. During the pregnancy, the doctors at Fort Campbell, Kentucky, didn't diagnose that she was pregnant. She was having abdominal and vaginal pains, so she went to the hospital. By her being heavy and having an irregular menstrual cycle, pregnancy never crossed her mind. One day, the pain became severe and she was rushed to the emergency room. She was treated, released and given medication to take at home. She had taken the medication as prescribed. While bathing, she felt a sharp pain. Then bleeding occurred. When the fetus pushed out from her vagina into the bath water, she was frightened and hurt, almost to the point of being hysterical. Composing herself, she took the fetus to the hospital. The fetus was a boy that weighted two and a half pounds.

Virginia felt so sorry for Hillary after reading the letter. Hillary said she was going to sue the hospital. After she read the letter, she decided to phone Regina, but her phone was disconnected. Weeks later, the Slaughter family left Ft. Dix and boarded a plane for Berlin. This time, Slaughter got a command-sponsored tour, which meant that his family could travel with him.

THE IRON CURTAIN

They arrived in Berlin, Germany, in March of 1987. The wall was still up. Their sponsor, who's responsible for getting them settled in the area was waiting for them. The sponsor took them to the Darlem Guest House, and they lived there for about a month before moving into their quarters. Berlin was beautiful, plenty of land and densely populated. The people were warm and cordial, though many East Germans lived in poverty. Once they moved into their quarters, Slaughter arranged to travel to Bremerhaven, Germany to pick up their car. He went by train. Traveling by train meant that he had to have flag orders, identification cards for each family member, vehicle ownership documentation and a passport. They had to be at the American train station (U-Bahn) at least two hours before leaving. Departure times were always scheduled around 9 p.m. and arrival times in Bremerhaven around 6 or 7 a.m. the following morning.

Each compartment cart had a couch that converted to a bed. Since they left at night, they had already prepared the compartment cart for night travel. Traveling by night through the corridor was the only way one could go through East Germany. This was mostly a deserted area. They could, however, view the highways and buildings of East Germany from the train. They saw their cars, which had motors the size of lawn mowers motors. The buildings had deteriorated and the streets needed fixing.

When the train got to the end of the corridor, Russianguardswouldcheck each passenger's papers for traveling. Once they arrived in Bremerhaven, Germany, a shuttle bus took them to the vehicle transportation office, where they picked up the car. On their way back to Berlin, they had to stop in Helmstadt (Checkpoint Bravo). While there, their papers for traveling in a communist country were checked. The Russians gave them a book with directions on traveling through the corridor. The book had photos of communist road signs reinforced with written directions. They had about two and a half hours to travel through the corridor. If you arrived in less than the given amount of time, they assumed that you speeded, and you were automatically restricted from traveling in the country by vehicle. If it took you more time, then they assumed you got lost, and the American and Russian authority in the area looked for you. During their drive through the corridor, they saw nothing but open farmland. The farm land, however, was not close to the highway. The area along the highway itself appeared deserted except for the other drivers (mostly East Germans) interacting with each other.

They were scared because they didn't know what they would be facing during their journey through the corridor. As thery approached the end of the journey, they had to stop at the Russian checkpoint. As Slaughter drove the car toward the watchtower where a Russian guard was stationed, Virginia's heart started beating faster. She could tell from the look on Slaughter's face that his heart was racing too. The children openly voiced their fears. The Russians told them to proceed with minimum speed. Once we arrived at the Russian checkpoint, they were stop by a Russian guard. Slaughter got out of the car and saluted the guard who returned the salute. The guard then pointed to where to go for further instructions. The guard continued to watch them as they sat in the car. Virginia immediately locked all the car doors.

"Mom, the guard is walking around our car," said Carlene.

"I guess he's checking out the car," said Virginia.

"Mom, I hope they don't do anything to dad," said Junior.

"Your father had to take those papers inside so they can check to see who we are, why we're here, and where we're traveling from."

"Are you scared, Mom?" asked Junior.

"Yes, I'm scared, but they aren't going to bother us. I just hope it won't take long before your father returned."

The guard remained standing, not moving a muscle. It was as if he was a robot. Slaughter left the building and returned to the car, again exchanging salutes with the guard before entering the car. The guard then walked away allowing them to pass as the rail guard rased the pole for them to travel through.

"Virginia, I have never been so scared in all my life. They were friendly. I gave them my paperwork. One of the guards asked me for a souvenir, but I didn't have anything. We were briefed not to exchange any items anyway. Honey, I can't imagine wearing those uniforms and standing in the cold like that. I will say that they're dressed for the weather. Are you alright? We can relax now. All I have to do is to turn in this book at Checkpoint Bravo then we are in Berlin."

When they reached Checkpoint Bravo in West Berlin, they thanked god for a safe return. Virginia went to East Berlin to shop. There was only one entering and exiting point into East Berlin called: Checkpoint Charlie. At this point, you would see the sign that said, "You are now leaving the American Sector." They check you again for the proper papers needed for traveling into a communist country. Everyone lived at the same level in East Berlin. They received the same monthly income of one thousand east marks. It took an East German ten years to purchase a car. The buildings were very old, some needing interior and exterior repair. The streets needed extensive road repair. The main shopping area, Alexander Platz, was the most popular shop-till-you-drop conglomeration of stores. Americans did most of their shopping there. The Centrum also was popular as well as some of their specialty boutiques. Americans shopped for crystal, china, porcelain, feather deckers, nutcrackers, and clothing. The dollar reigned supreme in East Germany. Merchandise was cheap.

Infants were not allowed inside the stores. They had to stay outside in their baby carriages alone and unattended. To see a carriage outside with a baby was common. The stores would close every day from twelve until three o'clock in the afternoon, reopening from three until closing. The restaurants remained open. West Berlin, however, was like living in New York City, though smaller. It had modern facilities and tall buildings. The Kurtfursadamn Strasser was the main shopping street for tourists. The value of the dollar was very low. Merchandise was expensive. Nevertheless, the city was beautiful. The food was tasteful and the people were warm. The Slaughter family befriended many Germans while living there.

ESCALATING TURMOILS

One evening, The Morgan's invited Virginia and Slaughter to a cook out. Virginia asked Sabrina Mills, a girlfriend who also was the director of the Army Community Service to attend. Sabrina was reluctant to come at first until Virginia assured her that it was okay. And it would give her the opportunity to meet people, since she was single. Sabrina worked there as a civilian employer. Sabrina was enjoying herself at the cook out; she got the opportunity to meet many people. Unfortunately, she hadn't met any single men since everyone there was married. The evening winded down and people started leaving. A friend of Vera Morgan's, Clyde Knead, offered to take Sabrina home since he was going that way. Virginia asked his wife, Barbara, if he was alright. Barbara, who was friendly and homely, immediately said, "Sure, it's okay." So Virginia told Sabrina about the offer and if she minded riding with them.

"Sure, that way I don't have to worry about you driving home by yourself, since Slaughter's been drinking and can't drive or ride with you," said Sabrina. She called Virginia the next day and told her that Knead had stopped by that evening. He told her, he was in the area and wanted to check to see how she was doing. She told him she wasn't dressed and that she was fine and thanked him for dropping by.

"Virginia, I don't know what this man's intentions are, but I don't mess around with married men. I'm looking for a single man." Sabrina lived in the Officer Guest House until her quarters came through. Knead started playing the slots machines at the guest house as an excuse to visit Sabrina. Sabrina always called Virginia when Knead came by, and she always refused to invite him in. Then Knead decided to stop by her job, she told Virginia how he would proposition her. One day, Sabrina called and said she was walking to the bus stop when her shoe heel broke. Knead saw her, honked, and pulled over and offered her a ride home, which she accepted. While driving, he talked about his marriage. Sabrina said that she told him to try to work it out, especially since they have a child. When they arrived at the Officer Guest House Sabrina thanked him for the ride, but Knead said, "I'd rather have a kiss instead."

"I can't wait until I get quarters. At least he won't know where I'm staying and use the casino area of the club as an excuse for hanging around." Sabrina eventually got quarters and saw less of Knead. While working at the Civilian Personnel Office, Virginia ran into Knead. He asked about Sabrina. Virginia said that she was doing fine, being careful not to mention where she was staying. Virginia noticed that Knead constantly came by the office to see Rosalyn Freeman, claiming that he was getting some information for his wife. Others there could have helped him, but he insisted on Rosalyn. Virginia took Rosalyn to lunch one day (Rosalyn was pregnant at the time), and they ran into Knead. Knead pulled up a chair and joined them at the snack bar. Virginia couldn't help but notice how his eyes glowed every time he looked at Rosalyn. He asked, "When are you due?"

"Anytime now," she answered.

Knead's bald head glistened as he smiled and said, "Let me know when you have the baby."

The next day, Rosalyn's husband, Gary, called his wife's job and said that she was in the hospital and had given birth to a boy. Later that day, Knead dropped by the office and asked about Rosalyn. Virginia related the news to him, and he said, "Barbara, and I will bring her a card and some flowers."

Virginia took a card and a gift for the baby to Rosalyn after work. Rosalyn was happy to see her and mentioned that Knead came by. "Rosalyn, I don't care what you say. Knead has the likes for you."

"We're just friends, and he's only trying to help his wife find a better job. Besides, Barbara came too."

"Okay, if you say so, but don't say that I didn't warn you."

A couple of months passed, and Rosalyn got a new job at the Rehabilitation Treatment Facility. Virginia also got another job working at the Army Community Service with Sabrina.

Slaughter had reservations about his wife's new job, especially since it paid more money. He started drinking more. Virginia began to focus all her energy on the children and her new job. Every evening Slaughter came home, he got drunk. Virginia openly disapproved of his drinking. So he decided going to Vera's house (who stayed below them) to get his drinks. When she would tell Slaughter to stop drinking, he would say that he was going to drink until the day he died. Virginia told Rosalyn about her husband's alcohol problem. "I hate to go home after work. All he does is drink. He doesn't drink hard liquor every night, but he does drink at least two six packs of beer a night."

"Virginia, you might want to consider getting Slaughter some help," Rosalyn offered.

The Slaughter's had requested the released of their household goods that had finally arrived in Berlin, Germany. They had a lot of damage to submit for reimbursement. Virginia was very upset that their furniture had been damaged, especially the items that they bought from Japan. They submitted their claim to the Finance and Accounting Office. The captain was reluctant to accept the claim they submitted and decided to handle it personally. He came out to see the damage himself. Once there, it surprised him to see that a black family actually once had all they had claimed to have lost. And that the damage did occur during shipment. Still, the army didn't adequately compensate them for the items, nor were they given enough money to replace them. Virginia had to replace the items, she loved them. She silently thanked God for her job. They had three living room sets destroyed by the military moving companies during Slaughter's military career. As soon they would get on their feet and strive for something else, Uncle Sam would relocate them somewhere else.

"Lord, are we ever going to breathe from bills?" Virginia said, looking at her damage furniture.

Rosalyn came by to ask Virginia to work at the Volksfeast for a couple of nights. The damage done to the Slaughter's furniture surprised her also, and she offered moral support to her friend. "Slaughter has to be as upset as you are."

"He tries to drink his problems away while I worry about how were going to replace the furniture."

"Don't you worry about it. If he doesn't want nice things, then don't you worry about getting them either."

"I can't stand to have my children not having something nice in their home to make them proud of because of their father's problem."

"That's why you should consider getting him some help. You can't go on like this much longer. Why don't you attend the al-non meeting?" Rosalyn asked. At an al-non meeting, it surprised Virginia to learn she may have contributed to her husband's drinking problem. They told her she was a co-alcoholic: A person who enables an alcoholic to drink. She decided from this first meeting that she would attend more often. Slaughter noticed a change in his wife. The nagging stopped. She allowed him to sleep through the night on the sofa without waking him to go to bed. He began being late for work and Virginia refused to call in with an excuse. This didn't stop Slaughter. He simply relied on his daughter to make the calls or made up an excuse himself. Virginia decided to work at the feast. The feast is the time of year when Germans and Americans share their different cultures: food, beer, entertainment, rides, and language.

Rosalyn was very upset that night about something. Her behavior made Virginia nervous, but she could tell that Rosalyn didn't want to say what was bothering her. And she didn't ask.

Slaughter picked Virginia up after the feast. As they were leaving the parking lot, Rosalyn waived them down and asked, "Can I get a ride with you guys?"

"Sure, you can," Virginia told her. Rosalyn's body shook, and she appeared hysterical about something. As Slaughter exited the parking lot, Rosalyn broke down and cried.

"I know I shouldn't be telling y'all this, and y'all may not believe what I'm going to tell you, but Sergeant Knead attacked me today."

"What do you mean you were attacked by Sergeant Knead?" asked Virginia.

"I was on my way to lunch when Knead approached and grabbed me in the hallway, pinned me to the wall, and French kissed me. I immediately pulled away and walked off. And a few minutes ago, he came to my booth and asked me if I needed a ride. I'm going to tell Gary when I get home. Then we are going to go to the Military Police Station and file charges. I can't live like this."

"I told you that Knead liked you a while back, but I had no ideal he could do this. Chill, Girlfriend, it'll be alright. Are you sure he did this?"

"Positive! Weren't I there? I can't help thinking that he's going to try something again, unless I do something. I'm afraid to go to work now."

"I agree with you, but you better be sure you want to put yourself through this. Knead has many friends and don't look like the type to force himself upon someone."

"Well, he did! And I'm going to tell the police!"

"Gary will be furious when he hears this. He'll probably want to knock the guy's lights out. I know I'd want to kill someone who had done that to my wife," Slaughter added.

"Thanks for the ride," Rosalyn said as Slaughter pulled into Roz and Gary's driveway.

"Now, you call me if you need me for anything," said Virginia.

While driving home, Slaughter said, "If Knead did do this, he can kiss his career good-bye. The military doesn't play with assaulting another soldier's wife or assaulting anyone for that matter."

At work, Virginia received a call from Rosalyn. She told her that she had told her husband about the incident last night. As expected he was furious, so they went to the MP Station. Gary was very supportive and encouraged her to report the incident. "They're going to arrest and file charges against him today," Rosalyn said.

"I'm glad everything is working out for you."

"Well, I'm going to let you get back to work. I'll talk to you later."

A few minutes later, Virginia gets a call from Barbara Knead. She was angry, saying that Rosalyn and Gary had file charges against her husband. "What did your husband do?" Virginia asked, not letting on that she knew what the big commotion was about.

"He didn't do it, but Rosalyn is saying that Knead assaulted her."

"You mean he hit her?" Virginia questioned, still pretending not to know what was going on.

"No! Rosalyn said that Clyde forced her against a wall and French kissed her. Girl, she's lying. Clyde would never do anything like that. When she was in the hospital having her baby, we took her a card and some flowers."

"Don't get yourself all upset over this. The truth will come out. And, I'm sure the court will cleare Clyde of these charges."

"Virginia, I called you because you're their friend. I was hoping you could fill me in on why they're doing this to us."

"I have no idea what's going on, but I do want to say this; I don't want to be in the middle of this mess. I'm fond of both of you and I won't allow myself to get sandwiched. Now, I know that you may find it difficult to accept me still being friends with Rosalyn. However, Rosalyn and I were friends long before you and me, though I met you before her."

"I still want us to be friends, too. I just don't know why she would lie about Clyde."

"I got to hang up, I have a call waiting," said Virginia.

After answering the call, Sabrina came by Virginia's desk and could tell that something was on her mind.

"I don't mean to pry but is something wrong between you and Slaughter?" asked Sabrina.

"Oh, no, I wish that was it, but, no, that's not it." Virginia signed and said, "You are going to hear about it anyway. Clyde Knead assaulted Rosalyn Freeman at work yesterday."

"He did what?"

"He grabbed her in the hallway and forced her to French kiss him."

"You know how I feel about Clyde, he was after me too. I had to pull my scissors out on him in my office one day."

"What? You never told me that!"

"He made me feel like I had to defend myself. Girl, he made up some excuse for coming by. I had already told him that I had no interest in his bald-headed, four-eyed ass. I thought I had made it clear, how I felt about him coming here. Then he tried to grab me from the other side of my desk. That's when I got my scissors and threaten to use them if he didn't leave me alone. I haven't seen him since. Please don't mention this to anyone. I don't won't to be involved. I handled Knead when he came on to me."

"But how about Rosalyn? The man assaulted her! If you came forward with this information, they would surely put him away."

"I can't take that risk. I'm a single woman, plus I don't won't to jeopardize my career by getting involved. My name will be all over. People might even say I encouraged it. At least Rosalyn has a husband. I have no one to stand by me."

"I promise not to mention a word. This gives me something else to keep silent about that could help another one of my friends." *Why do people choose to confide in me?* Virginia asked herself.

The Knead case was hot. More information came out during the investigation. Apparently, Knead had assaulted some teenagers who worked as summer help at his company. They came forward with their stories. Knead's case didn't look too good, even his friends began to have doubts about him. One day, after school, Carlene told her mother that a student in her class said that she had to testify at Sergeant Knead's trial.

"Baby, it is true. Mrs. Rosalyn charged Sergeant Knead with assault."

Carlene's revelation made Virginia angry. She insinuated that Knead must be a real live maniac. He even victimized students. *It could have been my daughter,* she thought as she reflected on how close her family had been with the Kneads. Knead's trial began a couple of months later. The proceedings drained Rosalyn and Gary. It was a trying time for both of them. Concerned and believing that Knead was guilty, Virginia revealed Sabrina's secret to Rosalyn. It deviated Rosalyn to learn that Sabrina was a victim of Knead's but refused to come forward with the information. Virginia told her to call Sabrina first before telling her she knew of the confrontation she had with Knead. Sabrina could always deny that it happened. Rosalyn confronted Sabrina with the information and pleaded with her to come forward and testify. She still refused.

"I know now to whom your loyalty lies." Virginia said, trying to explain that she felt she did the right thing though she betrayed a friend in the process. Virginia was willing to sacrifice her job to see justice served. Sabrina didn't accept Virginia resignation, because Virginia was doing an outstanding job. Besides this was personal, not professional and Sabrina could distinguish between the two. As far as their friendship went, Sabrina didn't feel that they had a friendly relationship anyway. The trial went on and the court found Knead guilty of all charges and sent him to prison. The military court busted him from a staff sergeant with fifteen years of service to a private. The military court sentenced him to several months in prison. The outcome of her husband's trial had Barbara in a state of shock. She swore that Rosalyn will, one day, pay for what she had done. While her husband served his time in Fort Leavenworth Prison, Barbara and their baby returned to the states. Rosalyn was glad and proud of the students whom came forward with their stories. She knew that it was difficult for them as it was for her, especially having to relive the moment over. As time passed, Rosalyn and the students managed to put their lives back in order. Sabrina applied for another position in Bamberg, Germany. She decided to accept the position, especially since she had that experience with Knead in Berlin. Some say they're more to her decision to leave than she cared to admit.

A month later, a new director, Serina Robinson, was assigned to the Army Community Service. Virginia and Mrs. Robinson got along well. Though Virginia hesitated for a while before socializing with her superior, Serina was more professional, which made it easier for Virginia to maintain a professional relationship. Serina hired an assistant named Rick Johnson. He had some good ideals for improvements in the facility and, some idealistic techniques for the staff serving in the Berlin Community. Serina assigned Virginia to assist him in his endeavors. When she told Slaughter about her promotion, he became jealous knowing she would be working closely with a male. He surprised her one day at work, offering to take her to lunch. This way, he could meet Mr. Johnson. It surprised Slaughter to see that Mr. Johnson was good looking despite being an older guy. Slaughter's behavior toward Virginia changed. He watched her as she dressed for work, making suggestions, and even forbidding her to wear certain clothes. Virginia decided that she wasn't about to allow him to control her this way. She felt that she had always dressed professionally and in good taste.

She decided she needed to see Rosalyn. She met with her in her office one day after work. She told her about Slaughter's behavior, saying he was becoming impossible to live with. "He drinks until he passes out and accuses Carlene, Junior, and me of doing all sorts of things. He leaves his beer in freezer and accuses us of spilling it. He leaves the stove on, burning his food and my pots. And he hits Carlene and Junior when he's been drinking."

"Virginia, its time that you made an appointment to see a counselor who can show you how to get treatment for co-alcoholic family members before it's too late. Slaughter's drinking could lead to violence."

"I need some time to think this through. I don't want to cause him to lose his career."

"Damn his career! I'm concerned about you and your children's safety. You all are living in hell. You think Slaughter cares for you and the children. All Slaughter cares about is having a drink. Don't wait until a tragedy happens before you decide to get help. Believe me, it's sometimes when an alcoholic has hit bottom, meaning tragedy, involving the family, before help arrives. Time's running out, Virginia, you have to think of yourself and your children, not Slaughter. Believe me, he's out for himself. Only he can help himself, and your support could encourage him to do so. Take that stand right now before it's too late," Rosalyn pleaded.

Crying and shaking, Virginia asked Rosalyn for the counselor number. Giving her the number, Rosalyn pleaded again for her to call if the situation got out of control. Returning home, Virginia, sees the liquor bottle and the beer cans on the table. Slaughter had been drinking again. Carlene was in her room and Junior watched television in the living room. At bedtime, Virginia put her nightclothes on and left Slaughter in his usual place—passed out on the sofa. She checked the doors and turned off the lights before going to her bedroom and falling asleep. Hours later, Virginia heard a crashing sound in the kitchen. She got out of bed and ran to the kitchen. Slaughter had broken the water pitcher trying to put a six pack of beer in the refrigerator.

Virginia exploded and cursed her husband out for his clumsiness and being drunk. Slaughter grabbed her and slapped her hard across the face. Breaking away, she ran to the bedroom and laid across the bed. She heard Slaughter call someone. Minutes later, he came to the bedroom and gave her the telephone. It was her sister on the phone. She said that Slaughter had call to tell her that she was ill.

"I'm doing alright now."

"Are you sure? You don't sound good at all," said Tricia.

"I just need some rest."

Slaughter snatched the phone. "She'll be alright, I called because Virginia's been ill and the doctor doesn't know what's wrong with her." He continued talking to Tricia.

Virginia realized that he needed some help. She went along with the bull crap Slaughter was telling Tricia because she didn't want him to go bananas on her, and she didn't know what his intentions were.

"Virginia never wants to call home when she's ill because she hate to worry y'all. I'll keep you in touch with her condition. I'll will take good care of her. Tell everyone hello," he said before hanging up the phone and going to the bathroom to shower.

She immediately locked the bedroom door and called Rosalyn for help. She was about to tell Rosalyn to make an appointment for her when the line went dead. She started to cry, she knew Slaughter had listened in on their conversation. He started bumming on the door, obviously very angry. "Who were you calling?"

Virginia placed the phone down and said, "I don't know what you are talking about."

Slaughter somehow unlocked the door and grabbed her, asking again, "Who were you calling?"

She was reluctant to say anything and tried to pull away. He threw her down on the bed and hit her repeatedly. She fought back and got away, only to have him grabbed and throw her against the bed again. This time her head hit the headboard. She grabbed her aching head, then reached for the lamp and tried to take his head off with it. He ducked and grabbed her leg causing her to fall and hit her arm against his barbells. She kicked her foot, broke loose, and headed for the front door.

She ran to Vera's and asked to use the phone to call the military police. Morgan, Vera's husband, went upstairs to talk to Slaughter in an attempt to calm him down. The children had woke up and were in the living room. Morgan told them that everything was going to be alright. Meanwhile, Vera was in shock and noticed Virginia's bruises and swollen wrist.

Minutes later, someone knocked at Vera's door, it was Rosalyn. "What happen Virginia?"

"Slaughter went crazy. He has broken my arm,"

"Don't worry, Virginia. I'm here now. He won't hurt you again."

"Her arm may not be broken," said Vera.

"I'm going to take her to the doctor. Who's upstairs with Carlene and Junior?" Rosalyn asked.

"Morgan is there with them," said Gary, entering the door.

The MPs arrived seconds later. Virginia told them what happened and then they went upstairs to see Slaughter. Junior asked the whereabouts of his mother. Gary told him that his mother was doing fine. In pain, Virginia screamed for someone to take her to the hospital. Rosalyn eagerly volunteered. At their apartment, Junior screamed at his father. "What did you do to mom?" Gary wisely held Junior back, calming him down, while the MPs questioned Slaughter. After the questioning, they removed him for the quarters and escorted him to the barracks.

Carlene and Junior packed a few items and went to stay at Gary's. The doctor admitted Virginia in the hospital. She had bruises on her shoulder and stomach and a broken wrist. The doctor treated her and assigned her to a room. They allowed Rosalyn to see her. Filled with hate, Virginia lashed out at Rosalyn about what happen.

"He wanted to hurt me. My God, how could I let myself go through this? Rosalyn, I want to see a counselor. I'm going to get help."

"It's out of my hands now. Believe me the general have received a report about this case now and Slaughter is in big trouble. I won't be surprised if they bust him. And they'll probably refer him to the treatment center, for his addiction, if that's what he wants to do. The organization he's with handles their soldiers differently from the other units. Their soldiers decide whether or not they want help.... I'm going to leave now so you will get some rest."

"Who has my children?"

"I'll keep the children until you get out of the hospital. Don't worry about them. You concentrate on getting better so that you can get out of here."

The next morning, Virginia's nurse gave her some medication. "Honey, I heard what happen to you. And I want you to know you're not alone. I hope your husband gets what he deserves." Virginia doesn't comment. She merely glanced at the nurse as she took her vital signs.

Dr. Brook, the physician assigned to her case entered and gives her a thorough check up. He also referred her to Al-Anon and the Berlin Community Counseling Center for treatment. The next day, Dr. Brook released Virginia from the hospital. Virginia called for a taxi to take her home. While waiting for the elevator, she ran into Slaughter. She was afraid to be around him. He told her that he's sorry. "I'm going to get help. I didn't mean to hurt you."

Walking away, Virginia went to the lobby to wait for a taxi. She later went to the legal assistant office to get information on how to leave the country. An official told her that either her husband or his commander has to request for her return. The worker also told her what she was entitled to in a legal separation. Virginia had visitors as soon as she arrived home. Sergeant First Class Dorsey who was assigned to investigate the matter came by. Minutes later, a Lieutenant Perkins arrived. They took Virginia's statement, and then told her what Slaughter had said to them on the night of the incident. They told her what could happen if she filed charges against her husband. They indicated that they would be supportive of her if she decided to file a complaint.

Virginia let them knew she had no interest in filing charges, but she intended to get treatment for her husband's alcohol problem. Virginia could tell from their questions they weren't interested with getting help for her husband. They were only interested in damaging his career. She asked the lieutenant to schedule an appointment for her with Commander Hopkins.

At the meeting with the commander, she emphasized that she was there because of her family. She wanted him to get her husband treatment for his alcohol problem, insisting that the incident wouldn't have happened if he weren't an alcoholic. Virginia said that though Slaughter could perform as a soldier, he was failing as a husband and a father. She reiterated that she was not seeking punishment, but support, so her family could recover from the crisis. "That's why I didn't seek help earlier, I feared for his career. There are others in the same situation as I," Virginia said, pleading her husband case.

Slaughter knew his wife was in the commander's office. He assumed she was selling him out. Unaware she was doing the opposite. The commander was happy to hear that Virginia intentions were indeed different. He said Slaughter was one of his best soldiers it surprised him to hear this as well as him admitting, not noticing the problem himself. He assured her that he would make sure Slaughter got the treatment he needed. He also promised to provide safety for the family until he completed his treatment.

Slaughter received an Article 15. Article 15 restricted him to the post and placed him in the Rehabilitation Treatment Facility Program. The commander also mentions how he admired Virginia's strength as well as her support of him, after what had happened. Slaughter called Virginia later that day. Junior answered the phone.

"Mom, dad wants to speak to you."

She refused to speak to Slaughter. So he told Junior that he was sorry, explaining he was sick and would be getting treatment. Virginia looked on as her son spoke with his dad on the phone. Although she had spoken to the commander on his behalf, she wasn't ready to talk with him. The hurt and the hatred for what he had done to her hadn't left. She realized she needed help in dealing with what had happened so she could get some perspective on how to deal with the situation without feeling angry.

Weeks had passed and Virginia had returned to work. Mr. Johnson was very understanding and offered to help if she needed him. Virginia was grateful, but she didn't want to impose on anyone. She was determined to fight this disease that had stricken her family through prayers and treatment. She regularly attended church. And also started seeing the chaplain for counseling that helped a lot. Her children were also counseled, so that they could deal with what had happened. Virginia and the children became closer. Their bond became stronger than ever, determined to fight the pain they endured from the affects of their father's alcohol addiction. The hospital had a Spouse Treatment Program during the final two weeks of the patient's treatment. They notified Virginia that she needed to attend these final sessions with her husband. This was so she would be aware of their behavior, and so she could learn how to cope with being the spouse of an alcoholic.

Virginia knew if she decided to these sessions that she would have to face Slaughter. This was a difficult decision for her. One she wasn't sure she wanted to do. However, determined to fight, she decided to go. A week before going to the hospital for the two-week session, Virginia and the children went to visit Slaughter at the hospital. He looked fine, and the kids gathered around him to talk while she looked on from a distance. He gave Carlene and Junior a checker game to play with while he attempted to talk to Virginia. He asked her if she would go to the patients' lounge so they could talk. She agreed and they went to talk. Slaughter told her that he knew it must be hard for her to visit him. He thanked her for coming and for agreeing to attend the spouse program session.

"Who's going to keep the Carlene and Junior while we're in the hospital?" said Slaughter.

"Rosalyn is going to look after them. I know you probably feel that she had something to do with what happened, but she didn't. She even sends her hello's, wishing you well," said Virginia.

"I don't hold her responsible. In fact, I blame myself. There's a lot I had to come to accept about myself and one is that I'm an alcoholic. I pray that we can overcome this. If not, I still have to beat this addiction, which I can assure you that I will. I hate what I've done to the children and what I've done to you. I can't change what happened, but I can get treatment so this won't happen again. Virginia, I love you and the children a whole lot. You may not believe it, but I do."

Virginia asked how the treatment was going. He said that he's doing fine and he had made some friends.

"It's funny, you wouldn't believe the people who have the same problem," he said.

"What do you mean?" said Virginia.

"There are VIPs with the same problem. You'll will meet them at the open Al-Anon meetings."

"Well, I've got to go, the kids have school tomorrow and it's getting late."

He gives her an unexpected kiss and she still doesn't respond. "When do they take your cast off?"

"It comes off tomorrow."

"Dad, I'll sure be glad, too. I have to help mom bathe and cook," Carlene said.

Hearing his daughter say this and seeing his wife in the cast caused tears to form in his eyes.

The day came for Virginia to admit herself into the hospital. She got a call from Renee Wilder, Sergeant Wilder's wife, a close friend of her husband. Renee worked as a dietician in the hospital and told Virginia that she would make sure she ate well. She also told her she admired her for doing what she was doing. She didn't know if she would support her husband if it had been her. They ran tests on Virginia in the hospital, including a standard AIDS test. Her room was down the hall from Slaughter's. He knew that she had checked in the hospital that day. Virginia saw Slaughter as she passed from the laboratory to her room. He followed her to her room and asked if he could come in.

"Sure you can come in."

"How do you like it so far?" Slaughter asked.

"I don't like it at all. I hate having to be here."

"Like you hate me?"

Virginia just looked and didn't reply.

"Well, I'm glad you decided to join me here. You know you can change your mind, if you want too."

"Why? Have you changed your mind about getting treatment?"

"Virginia, I have to get this treatment whether I want it or not; but you don't have to. Didn't they tell you that you can leave at any given time?"

"Yes, they informed me about the treatment requirements. You all are all by yourself."

"It's up to us to accept treatment. They just provide the method of coping with the disease and the medication for those who need it."

At the Friendship Club on Andrews Barracks, Renee and some friends of hers were enjoying themselves. Donna, one of the friends, excused herself from the table when Thomas Daniel enters the club. Thomas was Virginia's neighbor. Donna and Thomas went out to his car and she bought some hash and cocaine from him. Later, Donna came back inside. Renee asked when she returned to the table, "Where did you go?" She said that she had to talk to Thomas about something. Renee assumed that they were seeing one another. Thomas left the club shortly there after. Unbeknown to the girls, he had a business meeting that evening with some African and German drug dealers.

Thomas and the drug dealers exchanged drugs and money. They told him how well their business was doing and sent a greeting to his German wife, who introduced him to them. The dealers said that they hope to continue doing business with him. They also warned him what would happen to his family and him if he betrayed them.

"Here's a little something for your wife," said Cafe, giving him some free drugs for his wife, Lisa.

Thomas went back to the club and sat at Renee's table. Renee noticed how he mingled with the young ladies and the guys at the club; he was very popular.

The next day at work, Donna admitted that Thomas was a big time drug pusher, and it didn't take Renee long to figure out that Donna used drugs. Donna quizzed Renee for details about Virginia and her husband being in hospital. Renee, however, didn't give any information for their being in the RTF program. She did say that they were patients in the program. She felt that if Virginia wanted people to know, then she should be the one to tell them.

Renee told Virginia that she had some gossip to tell her about her neighbor when they had lunch. The statement puzzled Virginia, but she didn't concern herself about the matter. The Slaughters' first week of treatment entail group therapy, which included counseling with other married couples that were also patients. The women and the men had a couple of hours a day in-group sessions.

Melinda, a counselor, had her job cut out for her. Virginia was a strong-minded person. And Melinda could see that Virginia had a lot of hostility and anger inside of her. Getting Virginia to break would indeed be a challenge for her. She had the women to write an autobiography, and they had to give an oral presentation of it to the class. She used Virginia as an example of how a woman should groom herself, even under a stressful situation. By looking at Virginia, one wouldn't think that she had any problems. However, this alone wasn't enough. The counselor lectured on the different techniques spouses use that enables their husbands to drink. She stressed how they could change this enabling habit. The most difficult task was getting them to admit the anger and hatred they felt toward their spouses and to get them to accept the healing processes needed to overcome the hurt they felt. Once the women accomplished this, they were on their way to recovery.

The last week they focused on group therapy with couples. They were divided into individual groups of four people. In the women's group, Melinda drilled Virginia the hardest. She attacked her from many different angles. Virginia finally broke down and cried, admitting the hurt and pain and her true feelings about being there. She told the group she hated her husband. This was Virginia's first breakthrough into self-recovery. Getting her to face her fears instilled an understanding of the enabling role she played in her husband's drinking. This proved to be a major step towards healing for Virginia.

The wives' consoled her, crying with her, feeling a moment of joy knowing that Virginia had finally released the anger deep inside. Virginia felt good about herself. Now she could talk with Slaughter and others. She no longer feared being alone with her husband. The last week was the most difficult. The couples' sessions brought out the terrible problems that cause their tragedies, and brought them to the RTF Program. The Slaughter had learned a lot about themselves that neither were aware of. They learned how to have a discussion without it leading to physical violence, and they also learned what to do in the heat of anger. The treatment was outstanding and the Slaughters were more determined than ever to make it a part of their everyday living. They continued to attend meetings for support. They knew there were no cures, and that the disease was fatal. The use of the information given to them was essential to them having a happy, healthy, stress-free life.

Virginia and Slaughter reunited during their treatment. The hospital held a graduation ceremony on the patients last day. They gave the staff their thanks. Virginia noticed a slight change in Slaughter's behavior when she went to help him pack his suitcase. She asked what was wrong?

He admitted how scared he was to go home. "Not only do I fear going home, I fear leaving the hospital," he said.

Virginia reached out to him and said, "We are going to beat this disease. This hospital had been a safe haven for us both. Here, we had the assistance from the staff. We remembered the techniques they gave us for recovery and a true saying to live by: 'God grant us the serenity to accept the things we cannot change, the courage to change the things we can, and the wisdom to know the difference."

With these, they also gave us communication techniques, the twelve steps and support from community programs.

"The most precious thing of them all is our love for one another and the children we share. Together we can prevail," said Virginia, embracing Slaughter.

"Honey, you have given me the strength. What are we waiting for? Let's go home."

The Slaughter's continued to face their problems using the techniques they learned. Slaughter remained friendly with the people he met in the hospital. He continued going to AA meetings on regular basis. Virginia continued to go sometimes to the Al-Anon meetings. However, she devoted most of her time to Carlene and Junior, helping them to adjust.

The Morgan's moved, and Slaughter was appointed to the building coordinator position,which involved keeping the maintenance of their quarters building. Slaughter heard that Thomas got busted from a specialist to a private. Rumors said that he was a drug user and got caught with a lot of drugs.

One morning, Carlene told her parents she could hear an argument going on upstairs. Apparently, Thomas's wife, Lisa,was crying. Carlene said she heard furniture moving and the sound of objects slamming against the wall. "Well honey, said Virginia, you probably heard them fighting. I hope they can solve their problems."

A month later, the Slaughters were startled from their sleep, from another argument involving the Daniels. Slaughter got up and peeked out of the window. He could hear Thomas lashing out at Lisa in the parking lot—threatening her. The next day Junior saw Lisa getting on a motorcycle with a guy down at the shopette, a community store. He came home and told Virginia. Weeks passed and Thomas hadn't been seen in the building. They were late in paying their stairway fees. Slaughter told Lisa that they had to pay it by a certain time. Virginia saw Lisa dressed in a silk shirt worn as a dress and very revealing. She told her she was going out and that she will pay the stairway fees tomorrow. Virginia, who was on her way to an Eastern Star meeting, said, "I tell my husband what you said."

Month's later, Lisa informs Slaughter that the army was putting Thomas out. She told Slaughter when they would vacate the quarters. Renee called and told Virginia about a rumor that Thomas got caught dealing drugs again. The weekend the Daniels were to leave West Berlin, Thomas decided he was going out on the town. He wanted to spend his last hours with friends. Virginia and Slaughter heard Lisa yelling from the window, "Thomas, you shouldn't be going anywhere. You know we are to fly tomorrow."

That night Thomas and his friends went out night clubbing. Apparently, Thomas owed some people a lot of money. These people were drug dealers. Someone tipped them off that Thomas was leaving the country tomorrow. When Thomas and some friends were leaving a club, near the Kurdamn area, a speeding red Mercedes came from nowhere and went straight for Thomas who was crossing the street. The car hit him and his body landed on top of the car. The driver of the

Mercedes braked immediately, causing Thomas body to fly off the car to the curb. The Mercedes left the scene as speedily as it came.

His friends ran to call for help. The American and the German police arrived. They got a full description of the car, Thomas' friend said that the car had German license plates. An ambulance rushed Thomas to the hospital. The hospital notified Lisa later. He never regains consciousness, dying the next day. Renee called Virginia from the hospital and told her about Thomas' accident and death. After talking with Virginia, Renee went back to the locker room area and discovered Donna smoking hash. Donna was crying because her friend had been killed. Renee someone ran into him last night with a car. He was supposed to fly today. How can this happen?" cried Donna.

"Things happen and we don't understand why," said Renee.

"I bet his wife had something to do with it. She didn't want to go to the states anyway. It wouldn't surprise me if she hire someone to do the job. They said Thomas owed some people a lot of money and maybe they had him killed," said Donna.

"Well if that's so, the police will find out what happen. Girl, you know that you shouldn't be doing this. What if someone catches you," said Renee.

"I don't give a damn. There is nothing they can do to me anyway. Hell, the damn Turks and Germans always get high back here."

"Well, I just don't want you to get into trouble. Besides, this is a hospital, though we're in the dining facilities locker room."

"Do you think they will let us see him?" asked Donna.

"Honey, he's in the morgue area of the hospital now."

"I don't care. I still want to see him."

"Are you sure you are up for this?" Renee asked.

"It won't bother me if you come with me."

Donna and Renee went to the hospital morgue to see Thomas' body.

"Girl, they fucked him up bad!" said Renee.

"They sure did fucked him up!" cried Donna.

Renee embraced Donna and said, "Come, let us go now. There is nothing we can do."

Renee called Virginia and told her that they had seen Thomas's body at the morgue. Virginia couldn't believe that Renee could stomach looking at a body in a morgue.

"Girl, they messed him up. They fucked his face up bad and one side of his head was through. I don't care what nobody say, Donna was fucking Thomas. Oh, let me tell you this before I forget…Donna does drugs. Thomas gave her anything she wanted. Now, you tell me that she wasn't fucking him," said Renee.

"Well, you're probably right. Who am I to say something different? I don't know them, no more than running into them in the stairway when I'm going or coming and when they would come to pay their stairway fees," said Virginia.

"Well, I just called to let you know what's happening on my end. You call me if you hear anything," said Renee.

They held memorial services a couple of days later for Thomas at McNair Chapel. Virginia and Slaughter attended the services. Once they arrived at the Chapel, Virginia had words with Donna, Renee, and the other dining facility colleagues there to support Donna.

"Are you alright?" said Virginia.

"I'm fine. Tell me has Lisa left her apartment?" Donna asked.

"Yeah, about thirty minutes before we left. She should have been here by now."

"There they go," said Renee. "Look at her faking. She didn't give a damn about Thomas. She was fucking around big time," said Donna.

"Well, I just stopped to say hello. I'm going inside with Carlos."

"Okay, we'll be in later."

Lisa held up well during the ceremony. Everyone left the chapel and went home.

Lisa came over later and told Slaughter that she would be leaving for the states to escort Thomas' body home tomorrow.

"Will someone from his unit will be going with you?" Slaughter asked. "Yeah, they got someone traveling with me. It's a friend of Thomas.

I knew him, too, so that helps. I never had the opportunity to meet his people."

"I know you wish this wouldn't have happened. Tell me, what did happen?" Slaughter asked.

"Rumors says he was hit by a red Mercedes with Germans plates. So the police believes a German was involved in his death," she continued.

"That's what they are telling me too. Though, they're still investigating his death," said Lisa.

"I pray that you have a safe trip," said Virginia.

"Oh, before I forget, they extended my stay at the quarters until I find a place to live. So that's for two months rent. I don't know when I'm coming back."

"I'm glad they're allowing you all to stay in the quarters. If there's anything you need, just let us know. Carlene can babysit for you, if you'll like."

"Thank you. I'll keep that in mind, especially since I have small girls, one is still a baby. I'll see y'all when I get back."

Lisa returned to West Berlin in less than two weeks. She and the children did not live in the apartment. She apparently was staying with a friend. The friend was

Thomas' buddy. His family was visiting Thomas' family in the states. This was the same guy Junior had seen her with at the shoppette. Lisa told Slaughter that she hadn't found a place yet, though she was sure to be out by the end of the month. She said that her visit was nice. Thomas' family welcomed her with open arms, and she was looking forward to traveling to the states again.

"Everyone in Alabama was telling me that August is always the hottest month. So I'm going to be sure I make plans to travel either before or after August next year," said Lisa.

"Where are your children?" asked Virginia.

"They're staying with my sister. You have an enjoyable evening and thanks for looking out for my apartment."

"You let me know for sure when you move out," said Slaughter, escorting Lisa to the door.

Virginia went to her bedroom and looked out the window. She sees Lisa getting into Thomas' car with a young black guy and assumed that was Thomas' friend. Moment's later Junior comes home and said that he saw Lisa again with the same guy he saw her with before Thomas death. Gary decided to get out of the military in October of 1989 to attend officer school, hoping to return as an officer. Virginia hated to see Rosalyn leaving after all they had been through. She and Carlene accompanied Rosalyn to the airport to see them off.

Occasionally, Virginia bumped into Lisa at the commissary. No one ever knew whether Thomas' killers were found.

IRON CURTAIN IMPACT

On November 11, 1989, the Iron Curtain came tumbling down. The East Germans were now free. Forty years of imprisonment had now ended. Families and relatives reunited. The country was no longer divided and the people happily tore down the concrete wall. The Germans chipped away at the walls, hammering constantly. That evening, Slaughter and Wilder went to the Brandenburg gate where thousands of Germans gathered to celebrate. Checkpoint Charlie quickly filled with East Germans crossing the border. The streets no longer only belonged to West Berliners; they now were bumper to bumper with East German's vehicles. Slaughter and Wilder captured the glorious moment on video tape.

The following weekend, Slaughter and Virginia visited the border where the wall existed near their Duppel Housing area. They found more celebrating among the Germans who still hammered away, tearing down the Curtain. This marks a beginning for the world. The threat of the great communist country had ended. This event happened a few months before the United States Military started to withdraw some of its forces.

In Iraq, August of 1990, Saddam Hussein shocked the world by ordering his troops to invade Kuwait. This occurrence slowed the military's withdrawal. The Fourth Battalion devaluation was the First Regiment to pull out of Berlin.

Though there were rumors of others Battalion's, Iraq's invasion of Kuwait froze the realignment of the military forces. Units from all part of the Military Forces slowly built up their forces in Kuwait, preparing for an all out attack. Soldiers and their families feared how the situation would affect their lives in Berlin and worldwide. The military held special prayer services in Berlin post chapels for the soldiers serving in Saudi. The Masonic families prepared care packages for the sisters and brothers of their lodges and chapters. Free taxi service was given to and from the commissary for spouses who husband's got assigned to Saudi.

While preparing the care packages at the church, Virginia couldn't help notice Rhonda's behavior. Knowing that her husband Harris was in Saudi, Virginia gave her some help wrapping the packages.

"Do you want me to help you wrap that?" asked Virginia.

"Girl, do you know I didn't see you? I was sitting here thinking about Harris," Rhonda said.

"Have you heard from him?"

"Yes he called and wrote me before the war broke out. I just hope nothing has happen to him. I'm trying to be strong, especially for the children's sake. They need me now, more than ever.

Kevin and Cheryl are taking it the hardest. They're the oldest and they're very close to their father. Kevin tries to perform his daddy's chores, like making sure the doors are locked before going to bed, cleaning the cars and keeping the yard clean. They watch the news constantly. To me, that's depressing. I feel better when I'm away from the news reports. I can't wait until this crisis is over and all the guys can come home."

"I can imagine what you're feeling. I pray everyday that Slaughter don't have to go and thank god for moments that we have together."

"Girl, you know the saying that you don't realize what you have until it's gone. Well, believe it, that's exactly what I'm facing now."

"Well, we're finished now," said Virginia.

"Yep, we can all get our stuff and go. I sure did appreciate you coming over here helping me."

"I could see your mind was somewhere else."

"Yeah, Girl, it was. Thanks for listening to my problems."

"Oh, you don't have to thank me. I enjoyed our little talk. Maybe we can put this crisis behind us soon," Virginia said, ending the conversation.

More friends of the Slaughters receive assignments to Kuwait. Slaughter thought about Kuwait constantly, though he knew his unit would be the last to go to Saudi. Although the threat of war loomed over Berlin and the world, they went on with their lives. The Slaughter's tour was ending. Virginia and Renee toured Prague, Czechoslovakia in January of 1991. This was a critical time for traveling. International Tours Travel continues to sponsor tours, although the forces continue to build in Kuwait.

Two weeks after Virginia and Renee returned from Prague, President Bush ordered an attack on Iraq. Security was heavy in the American sector of Berlin. The American schools closed their doors. Army tanks were bought into the American housing area for use as roadblocks. Other vehicles blocked off the American schools grounds. The soldiers had to work around the clock guard duty to protect the Americans from terrorism. The Slaughter household changed. A different type of fear had them preoccupied: terrorism and a fear that Slaughter might have to serve in Kuwait. Fear of the conflict in Kuwait spread throughout the world.

Every morning, Virginia checks her car with a flashlight for signs of a bomb planted in the car. The guard at the entrance to her job would double check everyone who entered car for bombs. Buses, public schools, and military facilities were checked on a twenty-four-hour basis. Every military family in Germany watched television or listened to the radio for reports on the crisis in Kuwait.

Virginia received a call at work from a friend in Wiesbaden, Germany. Doreen's husband had been killed. Devastated by the news, Serina comforted Virginia when Doreen hung up.

"Did they know how he got killed?" asked Serina.

"They said that he had a heart attack. At least that's what Doreen told me on the phone. Damn that Hussein! He was only thirty-four years old. They extended their stint in the service last year because of money, now this happens. What is Doreen going to do?" yelled Virginia.

"You can have the afternoon off if you like."

"Thank you," cried Virginia, gathering her possessions. She phoned Slaughter and told him the news. Three days later, there was a ceasefire.

In Hanau, Germany, Renee's friend Ingram was notified that her husband had suffered an injury in the war. His right side had been injured from a bomb explosion. Though alive, he was messed up. His face, arm, and legs were severely burned, and he only had a small portion of his penis left. They had recently received their new assignment at Fort Riley, Kansas, shortly before he went to Saudi. Within months, Berlin returned to normal. For those who lost their loved ones, however, it would never be the same. The Bush Administration extended all the enlisted men military stints for six months. The Slaughters waited for their new departure date from Berlin. Within a week, The Slaughters knew they would be leaving in November.

Harris had finally returned home to Germany with the others who had gone to Saudi. Although the war was over, the military still needed soldiers in Turkey to secure the ceasefire. When Harris returned to work at the mess hall, the sergeant major told him that Turkey was his new assignment. He was furious and went into a rage, destroying the dining room facilities. The sergeant major tried to stop Harris as he called out for help to an assistant. Harris's friends ran to the kitchen and found him completely berserk and determined in his quest to destroy the dining room. Later, they rushed him to the hospital to get treatment.

Rhonda though distraught at hearing the news, understood why her husband had a breakdown. "He constantly had bad nightmares about his experience in Saudi. He briefly mentioned some details of his missions. He talked about constantly hearing weapons firing," said Rhonda.

"I have never seen Harris react this way about an assignment. This was too much too soon," said the sergeant major.

Upon Harris' release from the hospital, he found that his assignment had been cancelled. The Harris's were very happy to hear this. But that wasn't the end for Harris. The military decided to bring charges against him for failing to complete an assignment and destroying government property. This could mean the end of seventeen years in the army, only three years before his retirement date.

Rhonda was a nervous wreck. The thought of her husband's career ending—after all he had gone through—was hard to accept. Rhonda sought prayer with the chaplain. Those who were aware of their situation prayed too.

They hired an attorney from Frankfurt to defend Harris. He arrived in Berlin a couple of weeks before the trail to prepare his case. The Masonic lodges and chapters gave financial support to pay for the legal fees. Rumors spread in the community that Harris would not prevail.

The chapel had a gospel concert a couple of days before the trail. Rhonda sung in the choir. Everybody at church could see how upset she was the day of her performance. She even broke down and cried halfway through the song. But she continued to sing gracefully. The song she sang related closely to the trauma she now faced. The congregation joined in with their joyful voices singing with her. Her performance electrified the congregation.

After the service, Virginia and Renee gathered around Rhonda to congratulate her for an outstanding performance. "I didn't think I would be able to sing. But something inside gave me the strength to continue. Thank God it's over," said Rhonda.

"Do you need a ride? Virginia asked.

"No, Harris is here," said Rhonda. "Where? I didn't see him."

"He was sitting in the balcony. He came late, because he had to work."

"Everything is going to be alright," said Virginia.

Harris was found not guilty of all charges except one. He had to pay for the property he destroyed. The Masonic family sponsored a victory party for Harris.

In July of 1991, The Army reassigned Slaughter to Fort Jackson, South Carolina. The military sponsored low-rate tours for the soldiers and their families. Due to the desert storm, the Slaughters took advantages of the inexpensive tours. They visited Chimsee, Bertches garden, and Spain. Spain was a unique experience. They visited Majorca, an island off the coast of Spain. The climate was very warm and but not humid. Nude beaches were everywhere. Americans visiting the beaches were amazed at the open display of nudity. The scenery was beautiful. The Slaughters visited a pearl factory and seeing the development of pearls fascinated them. The people were friendly and cordial throughout the island. They enjoyed the beaches and pool areas. The nightclubs were very erotic; shows of dancers performing in wet T-shirts excited Virginia and Slaughter, who had fun without taking a drink.

Once they returned from Spain, they began preparing to leave Berlin and return to the States. They said good-byes to many friends. Virginia even took time to stop by the hospital to say good-bye to Melinda, her counselor, and some others. The counselor was special; she presented Virginia with the techniques to prevail any turmoil in her life.

This country had made a tremendous impact in their lives. Changes occurred that they would treasure for life. Slaughter received a Meritorious Service Medal Award from his commander: The highest award a soldier could receive. The Army commended him for his outstanding performance. He felt good about himself. He constantly thanked his wife for her support and God. They left Berlin in November 1991, for their new assignment at Fort Jackson, South Carolina, where they continued Slaughter's military career and their married life.